Luke

A SHADOW OPS TEAM NOVEL

Makenna Jameison

ISBN: 9798854815932

ALSO BY MAKENNA JAMEISON

ALPHA SEALS CORONADO

SEAL's Desire
SEAL's Embrace
SEAL's Honor
SEAL's Revenge
SEAL's Promise
SEAL's Redemption
SEAL's Command

Table of Contents

Prologue

Luke Willard ran across the cobblestones in full body armor, leapt over the crumbling wall, and dropped to the hard ground, rolling with the momentum. Ford Anderson was already beside him, tucking into his own roll with a grunt. The two men lay on the ground as stray shots fired from above, listening to an update over their headsets.

"Two tangos on the perimeter," Gray Pierce said in a low voice. "Both are moving north. I don't have a clear shot."

Luke clicked on his mic, speaking to the rest of their teammates. "We were made on our approach and retreated back twenty yards. We don't have eyes on the house right now but spotted the package. Repeat. We spotted the package. One woman confirmed inside on the first floor, tied to a chair. Over."

"You two sure know how to garner a warm

welcome," Nick Dowd said over the headsets. "Nothing like a little gunfire to let them know we're coming."

"Bad timing," Luke spat out. "No one expected that second mofo to be jacking off outside. He was supposed to be patrolling the perimeter but was watching the woman through the windows."

"Fuck," Nick muttered.

"What's her condition?" Jett Hutchinson asked over the headsets. Their boss had remained at the Shadow Security headquarters in upstate New York, sending the covert Shadow Ops Team to Mexico. Their mission was to rescue the daughter of a U.S. Government official who'd been kidnapped several days before. As former Delta Force soldiers, Luke and his teammates were every bit as lethal as they'd been when in the Special Forces. They'd deployed on counterterrorism, hostage rescue, and reconnaissance missions during their Army days. The men conducted similar missions now as part of a covert black ops group.

They just didn't play by the government's rules anymore.

"Bruised and battered," Luke said. "Torn clothes."

Gray muttered a curse. When the men had served together, Gray had been held hostage for three days during an op that went south. Although the woman they were rescuing probably hadn't endured the torture Gray had, she'd clearly suffered physical harm. It was likely she'd been sexually assaulted. She'd live with horrific memories of her kidnapping for the rest of her life.

"SITREP," Luke ordered.

"I'm on the east side, with my scope aimed at the

vehicles," Nick said. "If they try to move her from this location, I'll take them out."

"I'm on the roof," Gray said over their headsets, breathing heavily. "I scaled the building across the street and can see through the window above the entryway. One tango inside along with the package."

"You have eyes on the mark?" Luke confirmed, staying low as shots continued to rain above them.

"Roger. He's looking outside, no doubt wondering what the fuck all the gunfire is for. I can take him out. The woman is tied to a chair, and he's about fifteen feet away from her. There's also one lone asshole moving north looking for you two. The second headed west."

"Then we're a go," Luke said, nodding at Ford. His teammate gripped his weapon, and Luke made a circling gesture with his finger, indicating they should split up and surround the targets. He clicked on his mic again. "Ford and I will eliminate the tangos outside. Sam and Nick, prepare to move in to retrieve the package. Gray, take the shot when it's clear."

The man who'd been running toward Luke and Ford's hiding spot thumped across the cobblestones above them. They moved quickly, each heading a different direction to eliminate the remaining threats outside. Luke eyed the wall, readying to scale it. He and Ford had night vision goggles on and full combat gear. They were armed with military-grade weapons. The idiots outside seemed unorganized and unprepared in comparison.

"He's in my sights," Gray said smoothly. "I'm taking the shot."

A single gunshot echoed through the night as glass shattered, followed by the woman's piercing scream.

Nick and Sam were already running toward the house, and Luke and Ford fanned around the outside, eliminating the remaining kidnappers. By the time they breached the front door, Sam was untying the victim as Nick cleared the room and charged upstairs. Luke's throat tightened as he looked at her. She had a black eye and bruises covering her arms. Her clothing was torn, her lips swollen. She'd clearly been beaten in addition to being raped.

"It's all right," he said, trying to ignore the anger surging through him as he moved closer. "We're Americans. We're here to rescue you."

She looked up at him through teary eyes. "Don't hurt me," she pleaded. "Please." Her eyes scanned over his helmet, down his dark clothes and body armor. He wasn't in uniform because he wasn't an enlisted soldier anymore.

He frowned. "No one is going to hurt you. We'll get any medical treatment that you require and escort you back to the States. You're safe now."

"You're military?" she asked, her voice wobbling.

He shook his head. "Former military. We work with the U.S. Government though. You're safe with us," he assured her.

She seemed to relax slightly. "It's really over?" she asked shakily. Tears streamed down her cheeks as Sam carefully untied her wrists.

"It's over," Luke confirmed.

Sam stood, the ropes falling to the ground, and was already crossing the room and grabbing a blanket to wrap around her shoulders. Ford updated Jett over the headsets, and Luke's stomach churned as the woman tried to stand. Her bare thighs were bruised, the shape of handprints on her fair skin. He wanted to kill the men who'd sold her to these ruthless monsters, letting her be abused in the worst possible ways. Rescuing women who'd been trafficked never got any easier. She'd need medical treatment and therapy when she was back home. She'd be interviewed, but as many cases went, she might not even know much about the men who'd originally taken her. Sold her. Her kidnapping might be completely unrelated to her father's high-profile career, as no connections had been made yet. Jett had their IT guys scouring the young woman's social media and electronic communications to see who she'd been in contact with. It might turn up nothing, but they had to cover all their bases.

Gray came charging in the front door just as Nick hustled back downstairs. "Upstairs is clear!" Nick shouted.

"Can you walk?" Sam asked the woman, who'd fallen back into the chair, shaking.

"I…I don't think so."

He handed her the blanket and finally wrapped it around her shoulders himself after she fumbled with it several times, her hands trembling. "Is it all right if I carry you?" he asked. He was a large man, but the woman had seemed to calm as he'd tended to her.

"All right." Her voice was barely a whisper, and Luke scanned the room she'd been held in.

He clicked his mic, giving Jett an update. "We have the package. Three tangos down. Preparing to move out."

"Roger that," Jett said. "See you back home."

There were no sirens outside, and he suspected the neighbors had learned to ignore whatever dirty dealings were going on inside the home of the men he and his teammates had killed. Nick had already slipped back out into the balmy Mexican night to ensure the coast remained clear for them to extricate the hostage.

The woman whimpered as Sam lifted her.

Gray remained near the doorway, his dark gaze scanning the scene, his finger on the trigger of his rifle. Luke eyed him, wondering if moments like this brought back memories of his captivity.

Luke crossed the room on one final sweep, eyeing the dead body that Gray had taken out with a single sniper shot, and frowned as he saw a piece of paper on the floor. It was only partly legible, with spilled liquid blurring some of the ink, but there was a name and a phone number scrawled onto it. The U.S. area code made him pause. He snapped a picture with his phone and then bent to pick up a broken glass beside the paper. The asshole had been drinking and dropped it when Gray took the kill shot, the liquid smearing the numbers as everything had fallen on the floor. Luke slid the soggy paper into his pocket, to be analyzed further when they returned home.

"What's that?" Gray asked, nodding toward Luke's pocket.

"A name and partial phone number. I'll send it to the boss." He shot off a quick text to Jett, including the photo he'd just taken. Maybe the IT guys could get a head start, but with the blurred writing, he wasn't holding out hope for anything to come from it. His teammates stood by, ready to roll out, Sam with the hostage in his arms. Gray turned toward the door, aiming his weapon into the darkness.

"The outside is clear," Nick said over the headsets. "Head north toward me."

"Roger that." Luke signaled, pointing to the door with his gloved hand. "Let's move," he ordered. He stepped over the dead body, ignoring the mess and blood splattered on the ground, and he and his teammates exited into the dark night.

Chapter 1

Luke leaned back against a table in the pool hall on Tuesday evening, watching Gray take a shot. They'd been back from Mexico for two days, and he was still irritated as hell at the bastards they'd taken out. They'd briefed yesterday with Jett, and to no one's surprise, the blurry number Luke had found hadn't given them any useful information. It'd been a long shot, but the fact that the men who'd trafficked the teenager had contact with someone in the U.S. made him pause. The Feds would investigate further, but his team was done with their part for the moment. It was never easy when women or children were victimized, and his gut churned at knowing someone here in the States was still out there, free, possibly targeting other victims.

He took a pull of his beer, looking around. It wasn't too crowded tonight, and they had the back area entirely to themselves. He almost preferred it this way, avoiding the groups waiting for a table or the single women hitting on him and his buddies. He kept in good shape and used to appreciate the looks he'd get from the opposite sex but wasn't into bedding a woman for a night. Not that he had much interest in the type of girl that would aggressively throw herself at him either. There was something to be said about the thrill of the chase, and an easy lay didn't hold much appeal.

Luke smirked as Gray sank the ball right into the corner pocket, with Sam slapping him on the back in congratulations.

"Damn. He smokes us every time," Ford muttered with a low chuckle from beside him.

"Ain't that the truth," Luke said. "That's why I'm sitting this one out. I'm surprised you're even here tonight. How's Clara doing?" he asked.

Ford had been interested in the pretty receptionist at Shadow Security for months but had only recently gotten together with her. Things had moved quickly, with an engagement and Clara and her young daughter moving into Ford's house. His friend seemed happy as hell though, and he couldn't fault a guy for that.

"Good, all things considered. I love having them both living with me. It just feels right. I know it was hard for her when we were gone. Clara still has nightmares about Eloise being taken," he added in a low voice.

"I'll bet," Luke said, frowning. "How's her daughter?"

"She doesn't remember any of it, thank God."

"It's a sick world we live in," Luke muttered, his gaze scanning the few people scattered throughout the building. Low music played over the speakers, and a couple of groups stood around other pool tables. One lone guy sat at the bar, chatting with the female bartender. "I don't think I could stomach having a wife and kids and worrying all the time about them. I used to be pretty laid back, but some of the shit we've seen eats me up."

"We've seen the worst of it," Ford agreed. "But hell. When I saw Clara, it's like I just knew she was it for me. It made no sense, but even with trying to avoid her and not getting too close all those months, it happened. I couldn't keep away from her even if I wanted to."

Luke lifted a shoulder. "I'm not saying I'd push a beautiful woman out of my bed, but I've sure as hell never felt like that, like there was one woman I just couldn't get enough of." He took another swig of his beer, watching Nick move beside Gray at the table, angling his cue just so.

"Eh, you'll meet someone," Ford said. "If you're like me, it'll be when you least expect it. When Jett hired Clara, I never gave it a second thought—until I saw her."

Luke chuckled. "And then it was game over. I'm happy for you, man. She seems happier, too. More content and settled."

"You must've caught her when Anna's not around," Ford quipped. Anna was their boss's fiancée, and she was a firecracker. She was the total opposite of the quieter Clara. Anna had been brought onboard at Shadow Security to help run things at the large headquarters building hidden away in upstate New York. Jett seemed amused by her antics and was also completely head over heels, something Luke thought he'd never say about the gruff head of the Shadow Ops Team. Both Anna and Clara now knew the men ran secretive black ops missions around the world. The public had no knowledge of such things, believing the company provided bodyguards and security to clients. They lived double lives, but Luke loved the camaraderie he found with his teammates. They ran ops the government couldn't or wouldn't handle. As former Delta Force soldiers and teammates, they were highly trained and operated seamlessly as one unit.

"Hey, you guys want in on the next round?" Nick called out, looking at the two of them.

"Nah. I'm headed out soon," Ford said.

"I'd head out, too, if I was guaranteed to get laid," Nick joked.

"Shit, even if you had a woman, there's no guarantee of that," Sam said. "Have you looked in the mirror lately?"

"I haven't had any complaints," Nick quipped.

Luke shook his head as the guys continued to rib one another, not even sure why he was feeling out of sorts tonight. The latest op to Mexico had disturbed him. There'd been other trafficked girls and women they'd rescued on missions. Other horrors they'd seen. The partial phone number he'd gotten had been useless, most of it washed away by whatever alcohol had been spilled on it. The name "Ethan" that had been scrawled on the piece of paper didn't mean much either without anything else to go on. Something about it bothered him though, like evil was lurking. An American was somehow involved with the shady, evil men who'd held a woman against her will. Forced her to do anything they wanted.

"Any word on how that woman we rescued is doing?" Luke asked.

"No. I doubt we'll hear anything more," Ford said. "With her father a higher up in the government, they want to keep all of it under wraps. It sounds like we've got a similar mission coming up," he added with a frown.

"Oh yeah?" Luke asked, raising his eyebrows.

"I ran into Jett last night. Clara had left her phone in the office, so we went back together to grab it. He said there are several teenagers from Philly that recently went missing. One was found on the side of the highway, unconscious, but three are unaccounted for. The FBI thinks they may have been taken to Mexico."

"Holy shit. They were sold?"

"If not yet, they will be. Evidently, the girl that was found is in a coma, so they can't get any information from her. Jett was waiting on more info from the Feds before he briefs the team, but it sounds like we'll be sent in."

Uneasiness wound through Luke. Only recently, there'd been corrupt government officials taking advantage of underage girls who'd been trafficked in South America. They'd been arrested, and his teammates had brought the victims back home to safety. Meanwhile, he and Ford had been in New York dealing with Clara's nightmare.

"I wonder what kind of shady shit is going on now," Luke muttered. "The Feds have the manpower to rescue three teenagers. If they send us in again, something's up."

"Agreed. We'll know soon enough."

"Never a dull moment," Luke said. He glanced

over at their teammates, who'd started another game. "I'm gonna split," he said, pushing away from the brick wall he'd been leaning against. "I'm just not feeling the pool hall tonight."

"Yep. Same. I want to get home and see my girls."

"Say hi to Clara for me."

"Will do."

Luke called out goodbye to the rest of his friends, draining the last of his beer. A woman in a low-cut top teetered over to him in heels, but he nodded and continued moving toward the front door, brushing right past her. A night with a girl he'd never see again might've been fun when he was young and foolish, but sometimes he just felt old and jaded now.

He crossed the parking lot to his SUV, glancing up at the dark sky. He couldn't even see many stars with the lights around. Clicking the key fob, he climbed into his vehicle and scrubbed a hand over his jaw, feeling restless. He had great friends and an awesome career, but sometimes he still felt unsettled, like something in his life was missing. The trouble was, he had no idea what that might be.

Chapter 2

Wren Martin bit her lip, staring at her laptop screen in her tiny studio apartment. Her sister's smiling face looked back at her, but it was just Lily's social media feed. The sounds of the city outside were nothing but background noise, and she tuned out the horns and traffic, focusing. Wren scrolled through the photos her sister had posted—bikini shots, selfies, and silly pictures where Lily pursed her lips or posed for the camera. She didn't think the teenager should be sharing pictures of herself online in skimpy bikinis, but what could Wren do? She was Lily's older sister, not her parent. And their mom and dad had never been concerned in the past, not understanding how far and wide these pictures could be viewed or shared. They'd given it almost no thought at all until Lily had disappeared.

Glancing down at her notes, Wren tried another password to get into Lily's account. While there were comments on Lily's photos from hundreds of users, she had a feeling that whoever her sister had been communicating with had been doing so privately. She knew in her gut that was why Lily had vanished. She'd met someone she shouldn't have—someone who'd hurt her. Taken her. Wren didn't have Lily's phone to access her calls or text messages. Fortunately, Lily loved her social media channels. Wren knew she could find something here if she could just get into one.

"Here's hoping you didn't use two-step authentication, Lil," she muttered.

Wren tried a different password and frowned when it didn't work either.

Closing her eyes, she blew out a sigh. She needed to think. With too many failed attempts, she'd lock herself out of Lily's account entirely. The police had been worthless up to this point. She'd find Lily herself.

Standing, Wren crossed the apartment and made herself another cup of strong coffee. She'd been distraught when her sister first disappeared and the police hadn't taken it seriously. While they'd considered her a runaway, Wren and her parents knew that wasn't the case. But when three of Lily's friends had also vanished nearly a week later? Suddenly everyone was running around looking for answers. The police. The FBI. Probably some other federal agencies she was unaware of.

The disappearance of the teenagers hadn't been in the mainstream media yet. With Wren's connections, she could've called in favors when Lily first vanished and had it blasted all over the news, but she'd been torn. Would publicizing that Lily was missing hurt more than it would help? If her image was too widely shared, would whoever had taken Lily kill her simply because keeping her alive was too risky? Wren wasn't naïve. Whoever she'd been communicating with no doubt had horrible intentions. Lily was young and beautiful. Innocent.

The scent of freshly-brewed coffee filled her kitchen, and she was suddenly so keyed up and agitated, she wondered if she really needed more caffeine.

One of the missing girls had just been found on the side of the highway, unconscious. With three teenagers still missing, including her sister, it was about to be major breaking news. Wren was an investigative journalist. She'd already been tracking what she could of Lily's routine, desperate for any clues. Law enforcement had only begun their investigation, and Wren had pages of notes. Every minute counted, and Lily had already been gone for one painful week.

Wren crossed back toward her desk, setting the mug of steaming coffee down, and stretched before settling in to focus again. She had on leggings and a slouchy top, her dark hair pulled back into a messy bun. With her toned physique and long dark hair, she'd always gotten male attention wherever she went, but she didn't go out of her way looking for it. Lily was her total opposite—blonde and never without a spray tan, trendy clothes, and tons of makeup. As a teenager, she was overly into her looks, and Wren hated that all those pictures Lily posted had drawn attention from the wrong people.

She sank into her chair, taking a sip of coffee. Lily had always loved fashion and makeup and—

Wren quickly typed in a different password, letting out a sigh of relief when she finally logged into her sister's account. "Yes!" she whispered, elation filling her. She'd already been locked out of a different social media account a few days ago, but maybe now she'd get somewhere. She jotted the password down in her notes, a wave of relief washing over her. Finally.

Lily's last post had been the day she went missing, and she'd uploaded yet another sexy bikini picture. Wren had already seen the public comments on her photos but went to Lily's private messages. After clicking the icon, her jaw dropped as she scrolled through the communications from all the people Lily had been chatting with. No doubt her sister enjoyed the attention, but she had no idea that Lily had been talking with so many different men. It wasn't just texts they'd exchanged. She'd sent photos. Partial nudes. The bikini shots had been bad enough, but Lily was topless in some of the private pictures, her arms barely concealing her breasts.

"What the hell, Lily?" she asked out loud, even though no one else was there. Anger coursed through her as she scanned some of the messages.

I want to meet you, sexy.

Send me a nude.

I'd love for you to be my sugar baby.

You've got beautiful tits. I'd love to put my—

Wren abruptly stopped reading, her stomach turning. She needed to turn this over to the police. Had they even tried to get into her sister's social media accounts? Probably not. They'd wasted time claiming she was a runaway until Lily's friends had also vanished.

Clicking through the messages, Wren looked to see

if there were any men Lily contacted more than others. There were tons of unread messages at the top of her inbox. Wren scrolled further down. BigDaddy321 seemed to like chatting with her. She cringed as she saw the dick pics the jerk had sent. Did he even know she was underage? Gross. And why hadn't Lily deleted them?

PhillyT3R27was another guy she'd messaged a lot. Those pictures were more flirty than scandalous though. Thor69. Yuck. That thread was mostly shirtless pics from a middle-aged man. Why hadn't Lily blocked him?

Wren jotted down the user names in case she somehow got locked out of her sister's account. She'd follow up by checking out the profiles of these men and doing some more Internet sleuthing. Although BigDaddy321 wanted to meet, it didn't seem like they had. There had to be someone else.

Wren clicked on a message from YankeesE, realizing there were hundreds of texts in the thread. Bingo. Lily had been chatting with him for over a month. Although the early texts were just them getting to know each other, he was clearly way too familiar with her younger sister.

YankeesE: *You are so sexy, baby girl.*

Lilyx05: *Stop. You're just saying that.*

YankeesE: *I'm not. You could be a model you're so gorgeous.*

Lilyx05: *You think?*

YankeesE: *Hell yeah. I could introduce you to some people.*

Lilyx05: *Really?*

YankeesE: *Of course, baby. You're young and sexy.*

YankeesE: *I'll take you to meet a friend.*

YankeesE: *Send me a topless pic. I want to see your pretty tits.*

Wren froze as she stared at the picture Lily had sent him. You could clearly see her face, her lips puckered for a kiss, her hands covering her bare breasts.

"Damn it," she said, tears smarting her eyes. Her heartbeat sped up as she continued reading through the text string. This was it. She knew it. Everything she read just got worse and worse. A horrible sinking feeling filled her gut.

YankeesE: *Perfect, baby girl. You look amazing. I'll send it to Juan.*

Lilyx05: *He's a friend?*

YankeesE: *Yes. He wants to meet you. Are you in Philly? I saw that pic you posted at the Eagles game. I can come pick you up.*

YankeesE: *Send me some nudes. I want to see all of you.*

Wren wanted to vomit as she scrolled through the rest of the messages. Although YankeesE had sent a couple pictures of himself, she assumed they were all fakes. A quick Google image search proved exactly that. Whoever the mystery guy was, he'd stolen photos of male models and pretended they were him. Lily hadn't seemed to know the difference.

Had her sister seriously thought this asshole could get her into modeling?

The messages and photos continued, and her heart dropped as she finally found the meeting time. After talking with him for weeks, her sister had snuck out. This jerk had picked her up right from their parents' house, with both of them none the wiser. He'd promised to take her to meet his "friend" in the business. Lily had always been a bit wild, but to meet strange men online? She was only a teenager. Why couldn't she just hang out with the boys from her high school?

"Oh Lily. What have you gotten yourself mixed up in?" Wren moaned. She scanned over some of the last few messages again.

YankeesE: *Juan loves how sexy you are. He thinks you'll be perfect.*

YankeesE: *Tell me where to pick you up, baby.*

The messages Lily and YankeesE had exchanged ended that night. He'd confirmed the address, and that was that. Her sister had vanished. There'd been no mention of her friends' names in the messages she'd exchanged with the guy, but Lily had tagged them in many of her photos. It would've been easy enough for this guy to pull the same stunt with them.

Had all of them been in contact with this creep? And more importantly, where had he taken them? She jotted down the name "Juan," even though that wasn't much to go on, then clicked on YankeesE's profile, looking at his list of followers. Not surprisingly, most of them were teenagers or college-aged girls like her sister. How many had he been communicating with?

Her fingers drummed on the desk.

Wren looked through YankeesE's photos again, scrolling to the top, and was shocked as she realized that he'd been continuously posting photos over the last week. Her sister was gone, and he was out living his life. Carefree. Happy. On vacation?

Her gaze tracked over the pictures. The selfies were fake, no doubt, but was he also stealing pictures of food and drinks? Beaches? It looked like this guy was somewhere tropical right now. There were pictures of a crowded beach, a sunrise over the ocean, and an ice-cold bottle of beer with an outdoor bar in the background. They all seemed to be from the same place. He could've stolen someone else's vacation photos she supposed, or he could be there himself.

But where was Lily?

She clicked on his beach photo, poring over the background. No one looked like Lily or her friends, but if they'd been taken against their will, they probably weren't relaxing on a beach either. She chewed on her lip. Wren couldn't message this guy from Lily's account. She'd need to create her own profile to chat with him. Or she could go find him herself and demand that he tell her what had happened to her sister.

Her jaw dropped open in surprise as another picture popped up at that very moment. It was definitely a beach resort, and she could almost make out the name of the hotel in the background. Taking a screenshot, she did another image search. The name was blurry, and she couldn't enhance it without making it even harder to read. The distinct logo might pop up though. Her eyes widened as she stared at the results from her Google search.

YankeesE was in Cancun, Mexico, relaxing on vacation. Was Lily there? If he'd met her in person a week ago and suddenly started posting pictures from Mexico the very next day, had he taken her there as well? She scanned over the recent photos again, looking for any sort of clue. The photo he'd posted two days ago made her heart stop. The bottle of beer was the focus, but it was the hand resting on the bar at the edge of the picture that caught her attention. It was feminine, with pink nail polish, and she could barely make out the edge of a tattoo at the woman's wrist.

A lily.

Wren's heart raced as she typed in flights from JFK to Cancun in the search bar of her web browser. Her sister had been there, right next to this asshole. Lily hadn't updated her social media accounts and hadn't contacted them. Her friends were missing, too.

She'd been taken against her will.

Chapter 3

Luke swiped his badge and yanked open the door, moving into the secure area of Shadow Security. Jett had called an urgent meeting, letting the men know they were heading out on an op that afternoon. Luke strode down the hallway toward the conference room, almost bumping into Jett as he rushed out of his office. Luke caught a glimpse of Anna inside, looking pale, but Jett moved him along down the hallway.

"Is she okay, boss?" Luke asked, glancing over at him with concern.

"Morning sickness," Jett said. "I feel guilty leaving Anna alone right now, but she said she'll be okay, and this matter is urgent."

Luke frowned. "Damn. I hope she feels better."

"Me too. I'm used to finding solutions to problems, and this is one I can't do a thing about. Anna said it might last a few weeks or it might last the entire pregnancy. Time will tell," he muttered.

"That's rough. Ford mentioned the missing teenagers last night," he said, changing the subject.

"The Feds have asked us to move in. The media picked up the story. It might be local news for a minute but will be blasted everywhere soon. We need to move on this immediately and track them down. If their images get too much attention, it might be the last anyone ever sees of them. They'll be killed in a heartbeat or locked away in some basement, never to see the light of day again."

"Jesus," Luke muttered, swiping a hand over his jaw. "We just rescued a kidnapped teenager."

"It could be connected. Unfortunately, there's more than one human trafficking ring in Mexico though."

"We're headed back there?"

"Affirmative. I'll brief the team."

They hustled into the conference room, most of the others already convened inside. Sam came rushing through the door behind them, still in his workout clothes. There was a full gym, shooting range, and armory in the basement of the headquarters building. It made it convenient for the men to train and be available for new assignments. It also made urgent briefings like this possible to do in person.

"Thanks for getting here so quickly," Jett said, striding to the front of the room. He typed in his password on a laptop, bringing up his slides onto the massive TV screen. "My contact at the Bureau has given us the go ahead to move in on rescuing three American teenagers who've been kidnapped from the Philadelphia area and taken to Mexico."

"Shit," Nick said, scrubbing a hand over his jaw. "Three teenagers?"

"Affirmative. The first teenage victim, Lily Martin, was kidnapped one week ago. Three additional teenagers went missing this weekend, but one of the girls was found along the side of a highway outside Philly. She's unconscious and unable to provide us with any information at the moment, but all of the teenagers were friends. The Bureau believes a human trafficking ring in Mexico is working with a person in the U.S. who's been contacting teenage girls online, setting up meetings, and then moving them out of the country, either by coercion or force. He orchestrated the latest kidnappings."

"Damn. Why don't they arrest him?" Sam asked. "It sounds like they have the evidence."

"He'd hidden his tracks well, and they don't know his exact identity, only his online persona. New information has led them to believe that he's a high-ranking U.S. Marine with connections throughout both the U.S. military and government. They've tracked his profile in various chat rooms and seen the comments he's made online. It's possible he worked in Mexico before, either in coordination with another U.S. agency or as part of a military operation. The missing teenagers aren't his first victims. They've been monitoring the abductions and have been closing in on the possibilities as to his identity but don't have a name yet."

"They haven't ID'd him," Gray spat out, his gaze narrowing. "They need to work faster. He's victimizing underage girls and doesn't deserve to be in uniform."

Jett clenched his jaw. "Agreed. Given the contacts the Marine officer likely has throughout the government, he'd know if an official rescue operation is planned, which might send him into hiding. We don't know what he has access to, and we don't want him aware of the fact that the FBI is investigating his involvement. The mission is off-the-books."

"Understood," Luke said, frowning as Jett pulled up information on the missing teenagers. Their names and faces were on the first slide, and then Jett clicked to the next as he spoke. The teenagers had plastered hundreds of pictures of themselves across various social media sites, no doubt drawing all sorts of attention. "You've got to be kidding me," he muttered. "Their entire lives are online."

"Their lives may end soon if we don't get to them," Sam said.

"All of the teenagers were heavily involved in social media," Jett said. "The man who trafficked them has found other victims online in the past. Although the teenager found by the road is in a coma, authorities were able to gain access to her cell phone. She'd been communicating with him and expressed an interest in traveling."

"She went with a complete stranger she met online to Mexico?" Nick asked, looking at Jett in disbelief.

"She was going to. He promised her the trip of a lifetime and the chance to model. He's a liar and a manipulative piece of shit but damn good at persuading his victims to trust him. He uses fake photos and knows exactly how to lure them in. The FBI is trying to get into the other girls' social media accounts to see what types of communications with this man they may have had. Unfortunately, the first teenager went missing a week ago, and the local police didn't take it seriously, considering her a runaway."

"We've lost valuable time," Luke said. "An entire

week? Hell. She could've been sold by now and moved God knows where."

"We have lost crucial time," Jett angrily agreed. "Lily's family reported her missing, but the police dismissed it. Once several of Lily's friends disappeared as well, the authorities finally got involved and opened an investigation. The girl found by the road is Michelle Burlington, age seventeen. In the messages on Michelle's cell phone, they discovered communications similar to the man the FBI was already investigating in other cases."

"They don't have any idea where he is?" Ford asked.

"They don't know where he lives, but he's been posting pictures on social media this week."

Luke exchanged a glance with Ford. What kind of idiot managed to hide his real identity online but then shared pictures of his life and possible location? "What types of pictures?" Luke asked.

Jett clicked to the next slide, pulling up the profile for a man named YankeesE. Luke's gaze swept over the newest images. There was a crowded beach, an ocean sunrise shot, an outdoor bar, and more. Was he really dumb enough to document his every movement this way?

"YankeesE is believed to be the man in contact with the missing teenagers. He's also left a nice little trail for us to follow."

"Is that his hotel?" Nick asked in disbelief.

"Affirmative. He's in Cancun, Mexico. Although in the past his photos were more generic, he's getting sloppy. Overconfident. Using the information found in the background of the photographs, authorities were able to identify the exact hotel where he's currently staying. Upon arriving in Mexico, you'll need to go undercover. Find this guy. We don't have a photo of him and only minimal information. He's probably around fifty and nearing retirement from the military. The Bureau believes the girls are still in Cancun. The trafficking ring he's worked with operates several nightclubs in the area. It's believed the teenagers may be there, being sold at night to various men."

"That's sick," Nick muttered.

"How the hell does he even have time for this if he's a high-ranking military officer?" Ford asked.

"It's a good question. He's believed to be stationed stateside, given the fact that he can freely travel. Clearly, he's not deployed to the Middle East or stationed overseas. He's either nearing retirement with time on his hands or he may be neglecting his duties." Jett cleared his throat and continued.

"And when we find this prick?" Gray asked, clenching his fists.

"Find the girls. Afterward, do whatever you need to," Jett said with a shrug. "We don't operate by the same rules the Feds do. Let's end this."

"We don't need an arrest warrant," Luke quipped.

"Fuck no, we don't," Gray agreed.

"The human trafficking ring is highly organized and extremely dangerous. I've got dossiers on the ringleaders, background on the entire group, as well as information on their typical movements. We've lost time, but I have no doubt we can rescue the girls and nab him as well. The Feds haven't known his exact location before. He's getting sloppy, and this is our chance to bring that asshole to justice."

"When do we fly out, boss?" Ford asked.

"We're going wheels up at sixteen hundred. I've secured a private jet for the team. After our briefing, head down to the armory and get the necessary weapons and supplies. We're not going to sit on this. The news of the kidnapped teenagers is expected to break tonight. If their faces are blasted everywhere, they might be in grave danger."

Luke stiffened. They were already in danger, having being taken to a foreign country against their will. He wondered if the first girl was even still in Cancun. One week in captivity was a long time, and he hated to even imagine what horrors she'd faced. If the ring really did work out of nightclubs, that might make it easier to find her. It didn't mean she hadn't been enduring hell in the meantime.

The conference room door opened, and Anna strode in, carrying packets of materials. Her bracelets jangled with her movement, every piece of her outfit perfectly in place. She always looked polished and put together and was a contrast to Jett, their gruff former team leader and current boss. Somehow, they worked together though.

"I've got the information you needed," Anna said.

"Thank you, sweetheart," Jett said, crossing toward his fiancée. He brushed a kiss across her temple and murmured something in her ear. She still looked slightly pale but not as bad as earlier. Ford took the stack of papers from her and began passing out the information on the sex-trafficking ring as Jett spoke with Anna.

Luke's gaze slid back to the massive screen, where YankeesE's profile was still up. They'd find this bastard and rescue the teenagers, then end his military career. As horrifying as trafficking women was, this guy was also a disgrace to the service. If he was truly an enlisted officer, he needed to be held accountable and dishonorably discharged, then go to prison. It was bad enough when Luke and his teammates were tracking down terrorists, drug lords, and unknown enemies, but to go after one of their own cut deep. He was working in collaboration with evil men, foreign enemies who'd no doubt love access to military secrets. Even if the trafficking ring wouldn't use the information themselves, they could sell it. Blackmail him. What exactly was the extent of this asshole's involvement with the traffickers in Mexico?

"We'll find this prick," Gray said, looking pissed off.

"Damn straight we will," Luke agreed, picking up the packet of information that Ford dropped in front of him. "He doesn't deserve to be in uniform."

Chapter 4

Wren strode up to the oceanfront bar in her sundress and flat, strappy sandals, ordering a margarita from the Mexican bartender. The nonstop flight from New York had been just over four hours, with every second it took to get here agonizingly long. Now that she finally had a lead, she'd been anxious to look around, talk to people, and hopefully find the creep that had been communicating with Lily. She doubted Lily was freely walking around the resort, but she desperately needed to find her sister. Wren had left a message with the police detective assigned to the case before she left but hadn't heard back from him yet. It didn't matter. She'd find Lily herself. They'd wasted enough time as it was.

She'd conducted additional research on the plane, trying to find out more about YankeesE's online activities. Nothing that had turned up had been good, and the likelihood that Lily had been taken to Mexico made her blood run cold. Had her sister and friends all been trafficked? She couldn't imagine Lily running off with a stranger without so much as a word to anyone. Wren had dug into more than she ever wanted to know about human trafficking in Mexico, and that was only what was published online. Unclassified. She'd love to quiz the contacts she'd made over the years working as a journalist and see if anyone would speak with her off the record, but there simply hadn't been time.

The human traffickers were dangerous, with ties to several drug cartels as well. And as for the mysterious YankeesE? His comments and proximity to Philadelphia led her to believe he was American. Although he could've traveled from elsewhere, she doubted it. He'd been in the U.S. and targeted her sister. Anger roiled through her. What kind of sick monster would prey on young teenagers?

Her phone buzzed, and she pulled it from her beachy, straw purse to see a text from her best friend.

Ava: *You're where?! Tell me you did not fly to Cancun without me.*

Wren: *I'm looking for Lily. There was no time to text you before I left.*

Ava: *What?! You think she's in Mexico?*

Wren: *Yes.*

Ava: *Holy shit. Want me to come help you look? Whose ass do I need to kick?*

Her lips quirked, and she thumbed a response to her friend.

Wren: *Just got here. I'll give you an update soon. xoxo*

Ava: *Girl, let me know and I'll be there. Pinky swear.*

She huffed out a laugh for the first time all day. Ava was going to kill her when she got home. She'd believed just as Wren did that Lily hadn't simply run away. That didn't mean her best friend would be any more helpful than the police in finding her though. Ava was an artist, free-spirited, creative, and carefree. She wasn't used to sleuthing online or tracking down leads for a story. Maybe Wren should've updated her before she hopped on a plane, but Wren's only priority right now was her younger sister. She'd texted her parents and the police detective and hadn't looked back.

Laughter erupted from the beach, drawing her attention for a moment. There was a big group there, none of which included Lily or the other teenagers. Her gaze tracked over the people anyway, wondering if anyone was YankeesE. He'd been here with her sister. She knew it.

The bartender set a margarita down in front of her, asking if Wren wanted to charge it to her room. She told him her room number in a low voice, not wanting anyone to overhear. The bar wasn't too crowded yet, but it was late afternoon. People resting in the covered cabanas and thatched huts had waiters and waitresses bringing cocktails and beers right to them.

Wren didn't doubt that the bar would be packed this evening. It was interesting that YankeesE had chosen this particular hotel. The large resort was filled with solo travelers, couples, as well as families, which somehow creeped her out all that much more. How would she feel if she had children of her own, vacationing at a nice resort, with disgusting things like trafficking teenage girls happening right beneath her nose? Maybe that was why he'd come here. If Lily was with him, they'd just blend in with everyone else.

She took a sip of her drink, briefly enjoying the saltiness combined with the tequila and lime. She needed answers though and couldn't linger at a nearly empty bar. Wren took her drink, weaving between the tables. She wasn't above eavesdropping on conversations but didn't think that any of the tourists here were her mystery guy. She also wondered who Juan was. Did he live in Mexico?

A youngish couple were laughing and sitting at one of the high-top tables to her left. Pulling out her phone, Wren swiped to a picture of Lily. She approached them, holding up the photo. "Hey! I'm meeting my family here. You haven't seen my sister around anywhere, have you?"

The girl looked at the photo but shook her head. "No, sorry, I haven't seen her."

"Sorry," the guy said, looking back at his girlfriend.

"Thanks anyway," Wren said. The couple looked so wrapped up in each other, she wasn't sure they'd have noticed anyway. She doubted Lily was freely walking around, but maybe someone had noticed her the other day. If she was here, it was no doubt against her will.

And if she'd been handed off to someone else?

Her stomach roiled.

Wren didn't even want to imagine the horrors Lily might be facing. Her greatest wish that she'd been left alone up to this point. She couldn't stomach the idea of Lily being hurt or used and abused. Wren scanned the area, realizing she needed to come back later when it was crowded. She'd checked into the hotel thirty minutes ago and quickly rushed downstairs, determined to find this guy. The salty ocean breeze blew off the water, ruffling her long hair. She'd walk the beach in a few minutes, scouting out the area. Maybe someone would recognize Lily from the photo or she'd overhear something useful. In the meantime, she crossed the bar area again, deciding to show the bartender her sister's picture.

The guy was handing a Corona to an older man, who thanked him and then walked toward the woman he was with. She didn't get a trafficking teenage girls vibe from him, whatever that was. He'd barely glanced at Wren and was focused on the lady he was with.

"Hi," she said to the bartender. "I'm meeting my family down here. You haven't seen my sister around, have you?"

He glanced at the picture on her phone, pausing. "Not today, but she was here this weekend, right? How's she feeling?"

Wren stilled, her hand trembling slightly as she held out her phone. He didn't seem to be lying, and the fact that he possibly remembered her sister made her blood run cold. If Lily had really been here, where was she now?

"What day did you see her?" she asked, tilting her head. She slid her phone back into her purse, trying to remain casual despite the fact that every nerve in her body was now vibrating with anger.

"It might've been Friday. It's not unusual to get tourists who can't hold their liquor," he added with a shrug. "It's vacation, right? We usually cut them off so they don't make a mess everywhere."

She bit her lip and nodded. "Right. She wasn't with my parents then, was she? I'm surprised they'd let her drink that much," Wren added with a laugh. She flipped her hair over her shoulder, flashing him a big smile. The bartender's gaze tracked over her, interest sparking in his eyes.

"She might've been with your dad. Tall guy, kind of intimidating? He looks like he hits the weights pretty often."

"Right. He does like to keep in shape," she mused, her mind wandering. The man Lily had been seen with must be around fifty or older if the bartender thought he could be Wren's father. That only narrowed it down somewhat, because there had to be hundreds of people staying here. It was a start though, and more information than she had a minute ago.

"They must've been here before my shift began, because she was already pretty hammered. He had to help her back to her room."

Her hand clutched her drink more tightly. This asshole had her sister here in his hotel room? Was she still there now? "Huh," she said, trying to remain calm. "It was just that one time you saw her drinking too much?"

"I'm pretty sure it was just then, but we get lots of people coming through here. I could've missed her." A loud group of middle-aged women came into the bar area, heading over to order drinks. The bartender was watching them as well, and then his gaze tracked back to her.

"Right. Well, let me know if you see her tonight," Wren said. "I'll go look around. I'm sure they'll be here any minute."

"I'll let them know you were looking for them," he said, moving over to greet the new customers who'd walked up.

Wren's fingers were turning white from clutching

her drink as she turned away from the bar. Friday evening was days ago. If he really had seen Lily, what had happened since then? Wren wished she had some crazy awesome IT skills to hack into the hotel's computers or surveillance systems. She doubted anyone at the front desk would help her. She could probably steal a housekeeping uniform or something, but she had no idea where to start. The resort was huge, and she couldn't search every room on her own. She needed a room number or the man's name or anything. Would he come back to the bar tonight or head someplace else? Was her sister still with him?

Pulling out her phone, she texted Ava again.

Wren: *The bartender thinks he saw Lily on Friday, completely drunk.*

Ava: *Seriously? She was really there?*

Wren: *I showed him a picture.*

Wren: *Lily was in this hotel.*

Ava: *I'm booking a flight to Cancun. You need help.*

Wren: *Thank you. I'm freaking out. I'll explain more when you get here.*

Ava: *Text me the name of the place.*

Wren let out a sigh of relief, her hands trembling. She was used to doing journalistic investigations alone. To digging into stories, talking with people, and canvassing areas herself. This wasn't just another story though. It was her family. Her younger sister. If Ava wanted to fly down, Wren would gladly accept the help. Rushing off alone to Mexico had been impulsive. It was unlikely she'd just stumble upon this guy, and two people could dig faster than one.

What she'd do if she found them, she wasn't even sure. If Lily was drugged or hurt or—

She squeezed her eyes shut, trying to pull herself

together. One step at a time.

Wren walked out of the bar area, looking at the picturesque beach spread out before her. Kids were laughing, people were relaxing, drinks were flowing, and her younger sister was being held somewhere against her will. Helpless. A chill snaked down her spine as she realized both men could be here on the beach right now—YankeesE and Juan, the mysterious man mentioned in the messages. Her gaze swept from the beach in front of her up to the resort tower. There had to be hundreds of rooms here. She looked at the balconies, the sliding glass doors. If Lily was in one, maybe she could escape. But if she was drugged or hurt? Restrained? Was she even at this resort? Wren's mind reeled, not even sure where to start. She couldn't walk up and down the hallways, listening at every door. She couldn't stand there screaming Lily's name.

A man's booming laughter drew her attention back to the beach. She'd start here, focusing on the men old enough to be YankeesE. She'd scope out the bar again later. And if she had to, she'd find a way into those rooms, tracking down Lily herself.

Chapter 5

Luke and Ford walked to the outdoor bar of the hotel, surveilling the area. The place was packed, with music playing, glasses clinking together, and loud conversations filling the air on the balmy Mexican night. Their private plane had landed an hour ago, and the men had checked in to a neighboring resort. Gray and Nick were investigating the first club on their list known to be affiliated with the trafficking ring. The rest of the team was scouting the hotel in case YankeesE was there. They needed to cover all their bases, and if they could find this asshole, he could lead them to the missing teenagers.

Sam was already on a barstool, chatting up the female bartender with a beer in his hand. It was different than storming into an enemy compound, but they needed to gather intelligence. Selling women and girls was lucrative, and Luke hated that their mark had preyed on innocent, unsuspecting victims.

"It's crowded as hell tonight," Luke muttered. "Hopefully this asshole is here."

"He's overconfident," Ford surmised. "Sharing the photos of his location was the beginning of the end. We'll nail this fucker to the wall."

They walked through the crowd, looking around. If this guy was active-duty military, he no doubt had the standard buzz cut. They could eliminate any men with longer hair. Guys in their twenties and thirties were out, because it took time to move up the ranks. YankeesE clearly lived a double life with trafficking girls while serving as a Marine officer. The FBI profilers believed he was arrogant and a control freak, possibly divorced, and a narcissist. He craved attention. As his military career was winding down, he'd stepped up his new business, moving teenage girls. It was sick as hell.

Luke lifted his hand to his earpiece, listening to Gray's update. "We're heading to the first nightclub on the list. It's early, but a popular band is playing there, so it'll be packed. We need to make sure we get in. The leader of the trafficking ring, Juan Lopez, is known to frequent it as well. Maybe we'll get lucky and spot the asshole. I'd love to plant a bug on him."

"Roger that. You have the photos of the missing teenagers?" Luke asked, discreetly speaking into his mic. His gaze swept the bar area again. Laughter erupted to his left, but aside from a quick glance over, his attention remained on his teammate's update.

"Affirmative. Word on the street is that there are plenty of girls available here."

"Motherfucker," Luke muttered.

"I don't like the sound of it either, but at least the Feds know their stuff. Sounds like the list they gave us is credible. Now we just need to figure out which location the packages are at. Over."

Luke's stomach twisted at the implications of girls being "available." Ford didn't look any happier. Were they being forced to service clubgoers? To dance? Did men take them to private rooms against their will?

"I hope this sick fuck is still somewhere at the resort," Ford muttered. "I'd like to get my hands on him for trafficking underage girls."

"Agreed. He doesn't deserve to wear a uniform. I don't want to draw too much attention to ourselves by flashing pictures of Lily and her friends everywhere at the resort," Luke added in a low voice. "Someone might've seen them, but the American tourists will all think we're cops. YankeesE will split once word gets out, and we're closer than the Feds have gotten."

"Yeah. Let's see if he's around tonight instead. Look at him," Ford said, nodding toward a big guy with a buzz cut standing to the right of the crowded bar. He was muscular, with a tribal tattoo on one bicep, and he had several teenagers or young twenty-somethings with him. He tilted back a beer, his meaty fingers gripping the bottle.

"Looks too young to be our guy."

Ford swiped the pictures on his phone, looking from it to the teenagers they'd spotted. "And those girls aren't the missing teenagers."

Luke's gaze tracked around the space again. "That guy's too old—he wouldn't still be active duty, although he's physically fit. That guy looks like a bodybuilder but has the wrong haircut to be military."

"We'll find him—either here or at one of the

nightclubs. I've got a feeling he's still in town."

"I know. As sick as it is, I'm guessing he enjoys the 'merchandise.' I doubt he'll cut and run unless he suspects we're on to him. I'm going to see if he posted anything new on social media," Luke said, pulling his phone from his pocket. He'd downloaded the social media app before they went wheels up that afternoon. He swiped the screen, pressing the icon and watching as the feed popped up. It was weird as hell for a middle-aged Marine to be using the app, but that's where the teenagers were, and it clearly had served its purpose. He'd successfully found multiple victims. "Motherfucker," he muttered. "This guy was posting more pictures while we were in the air."

"No kidding?" Ford asked, looking over at the screen. The thatched cabanas weren't much of a clue given that they were all over the place down in Mexico. Luke hoped it confirmed that this guy was still around. He gripped his phone, swiping the screen with his thumb.

"Look at that one," Luke said in a low tone. Their target had snapped a selfie on the beach around sunset, showing the beach scene behind him but also part of his face, hidden by dark sunglasses.

"Hell. I wonder if that's actually him."

"Maybe. The other photos show his entire face— or the face of the guy whose pictures he stole. This is just his shades." Luke frowned, zooming in on the picture. "You see that? It looks like his reflection is in the lenses."

"Son of a bitch," Ford muttered. "You're right. Is he really that stupid?"

Luke pressed the download button to save the picture. "Apparently so. I'm sending this to West," he said referring to Shadow Security's IT guru. "He can enhance the image and hopefully give us an actual photo of the guy to work from. He can do some crazy stuff with his computer. It would make our job a hell of a lot easier to find him if we have a photo."

"This asshole is getting overconfident," Ford said.

"I bet he's getting out of the game soon—retiring, moving to Mexico. Or else he realizes he's under investigation and it's about to be game over."

"You think he's playing us?"

Luke lifted a shoulder. "These pictures have more clues than the hundreds of others he's posted. Maybe the guy wants to be caught. His career is over, and he has to realize that he'll end up in jail once this clusterfuck catches up with him. He wants to play us as we move in."

"Maybe he is giving them clues, expecting the Feds themselves to come after him, but to what end? Why give up now?"

"I don't know," Luke said with a frown. "Something's changed. But he won't be expecting a black ops team." They maneuvered through the crowd, listening to snippets of conversations around them and sizing up the resort guests.

"You can't get too much sun tomorrow. You're already beet red!" a blonde woman told her husband.

"We should've eaten dinner first. I'm starving, and the bar only has apps."

"All right, should we grab drinks here and then head into town and hit some more bars? I need to pre-game," a girl in her twenties told her friends. "Let's do shots!"

Luke neatly moved past them. None of the people around him were discussing anything of interest. They were going to have to start asking questions themselves, working the room. If they spotted someone that met the few characteristics they knew about their guy, they'd start up a conversation. Maybe he'd told others about the girls he had—bragging about his conquests, so to speak.

"Let's order a beer," Luke said. "We look too obvious staring at everyone."

"Nah. They probably just think we're on the prowl."

Luke smirked. The last thing he needed right now was to meet a woman. Gray and Nick were already headed to a nightclub. If the resort turned out to be a bust, he'd be hitting the local clubs as well. They had a list the trafficking ring was known to frequent, but the locals might have some suggestions. The missing teenagers could be in any of them or held captive somewhere else. Starting with the places known for trouble was unfortunately their best bet. They approached the crowded bar, joining Sam as they ordered beers. "Aw, come on," Sam joked, flirting with the female bartender as he pried her for information. "You can't be the only pretty girl around here. Where can a guy get a little action? You must know the hotspots that we should hit up while we're in town. Take pity on a guy, beautiful."

"You want some action, huh?" she teased with a wink. She slid two beers toward Luke and Ford, and he took the ice-cold bottle from her, tipping it back. The hoppy brew slid down his throat, and he watched as she leaned closer to Sam, her cleavage spilling out of her tank top.

"Yeah. You've got to know where my buddies and I can meet some girls. Come on, sweetheart. We're on vacation. We just want to have a little fun."

Ford leaned toward Luke. "Maybe we should start asking around, see if anyone knows about—"

Luke didn't hear the rest of what Ford said, because the sound of a female huffing in irritation beside him drew his attention. She was glaring at Sam, clearly overhearing his conversation with the bartender. Both of them were laughing now, the bartender resting her hand on Sam's forearm, but the woman beside him looked enraged and muttered something under her breath.

Her head swiveled toward Luke, and suddenly he was looking into deep, chocolate brown eyes that made his breath catch. Glossy, dark hair blew in the breeze, and the sexy sundress the woman wore made his heart stutter. It showed off her cleavage and slim, toned limbs. Her full, plump lips were pressed together in annoyance, but that didn't detract from her beauty. The woman beside him was stunning.

"Come here often?" he joked. It was a dumb come-on given they were both obviously visiting Mexico, not that he was trying to pick her up either. His mind had briefly short-circuited, however, shocked at the instant attraction he felt towards a complete stranger. She smelled both of coconuts and something floral, and as the ocean breeze blew again, he got a stronger whiff of her fragrance, making his blood heat.

She glared at him, like a bar at a beautiful beach in Mexico was the absolute last place she wanted to be. Her gaze dropped to the beer in his hand then moved back to his eyes. His fingers tightened around the bottle. He was itching to reach out and touch her, to brush some of that dark hair back and feel the softness of her skin, soothing that frown away, but she looked about ready to lay into him. "That's quite an original pickup line," she said dryly. "And no. I'm looking for someone."

"Someone like who?" he asked, pinning her with his stare.

Her gaze swept over him, and he felt his blood pumping through his veins. He was aware of every part of her—those dark eyes, sexy lips, and her killer body. He forced himself not to stare at her creamy cleavage but could see her chest rising and falling, the plumpness of her firm breasts making his dick twitch. She wasn't tanned or sunburned, so she hadn't been in Cancun for long. If he was the type of man into one-night-stands, he'd be persuading her to come back to his hotel room right now. Luke would love to peel off that dress and explore her smooth skin and feminine curves. Palm those luscious breasts. Kiss her full lips and touch her intimately until she was gasping, until he sank deep into her welcoming body, giving them both what they needed.

Her eyes ran over his muscled arms and broad shoulders, clearly taking note of his physical attributes. She cooly met his gaze once more. "Not you."

Luke chuckled despite himself. Something about the irritation rolling off her intrigued him. He was used to women hitting on him and his friends. She seemed entirely unaffected by Luke. A challenge. She'd given him the once over and barely reacted. He kept in good shape and knew many women appreciated that fact. This chick was the first who'd blatantly checked him out and then acted like she couldn't care less. "You're in a bar, alone," he pointed out. "Are you meeting a friend?"

"Nope."

"Don't tell me—you're from New York."

She raised her eyebrows, and Luke lifted a shoulder. "You've got the attitude, but the accent is easy to place, honey."

"Don't call me honey."

"I'm Luke," he offered, holding out a hand.

She blew out an exasperated breath but extended her own much smaller hand, reacting only slightly when his fingers clasped around hers. He felt it too, something electric at their touch that made him far too aware of her. "Wren," she said smoothly.

Luke held her hand a moment too long, enjoying the feel of her soft, smooth skin. She must work indoors, sitting at a desk. She certainly didn't have the calloused hands he did, nor the bulk. She was slender and toned but with curves in exactly the right places. Nice breasts. Rounded hips. He immediately noticed she hadn't shared her last name, but then again, neither had he. That didn't mean he wouldn't mind getting acquainted with her in other ways.

A slender hand brushed some of that dark hair back. Her floral scent floated in the air between them once more. "Your friend seems obnoxious," she observed.

His lips quirked as he glanced over at Sam, still chatting with the bartender. Ford had discreetly moved away, talking with another group of guests. His teammates were gathering intel, and he was busy chatting with the most beautiful woman he'd ever seen. He should be working the room, too, but he couldn't bring himself to move away from her. "What can I say?" he asked, his voice deep. "We're on vacation. He's interested in the local nightlife. Nothing wrong with meeting new people and having a little fun."

"I'm not sleeping with you."

Luke chuckled. "That's rather presumptuous, don't you think? I didn't even offer to buy you a drink." A hint of a pretty flush spread across her cheeks, and he couldn't resist smiling. She'd been snarky, but her reactions to him were interesting. Maybe she wasn't as unaffected as she let on. He wouldn't mind mussing her up a little bit, running his hands through that sleek hair and kissing those pink lips, just to hear her gasp. Pulling her body against his as he kissed her more deeply. He was working though. As attracted to her as he was, he needed to finish scouting out the resort and look for their mark. A gorgeous woman like Wren was just a distraction.

"I'm not looking for a hookup," he clarified. "I'm just grabbing a drink before my buddies and I hit the town. You can't fault a guy for that."

Her gaze landed on Sam again as his laughter filled the air. "Well, like I said, I'm looking for someone. While it was a pleasure to meet you," she said, her voice dripping with sarcasm, "I need to get going." Wren began to turn away just as a drunk man bumped into her, sending her careening toward Luke. His hand shot out to her waist, steadying her, and Luke didn't miss her tiny gasp as he caught her. She was soft and sweet, the frown on her face replaced by a look of surprise. He didn't let go of Wren, just enjoyed the feel of her curves beneath his fingers, and the sudden electric current arcing between them.

"Be careful," he ordered the drunk guy, who was already stumbling off. Luke's eyes landed back on

Wren's deep chocolate ones. "Are you okay?" he asked, his voice gruff.

She took a breath, not moving away from him yet either.

"Yeah, I'm fine," she said shakily, lifting her hand from where she'd grabbed onto his biceps and pulling back. Her cheeks were flushed, her lips parted, and her gaze went from his muscled arms back to his face. He got another whiff of her exotic scent as Wren brushed her silky dark hair back, telling him thanks.

"You sure you're all right?" he asked, quirking a brow.

"Yeah. I'm okay. Thanks for catching me." And then she was saying goodbye and turning away, despite looking slightly shaken. Luke watched as she moved through the crowd, graceful despite the fact that she'd been flustered by falling onto him. She bit her lower lip as she scanned the room, and he resisted the urge to groan. Her hair blew in the breeze, revealing more of that creamy cleavage where her sundress dipped lower, hugging her breasts. Something about her both piqued his curiosity and made his body take notice. She was sexy and spoke her mind, but he also detected a hint of uncertainty beneath the surface. A vulnerability that he couldn't quite place. He might be here on a job, but he'd be lying if he denied wanting to run into her again.

Chapter 6

Wren swallowed as she moved away from the man she'd literally fallen on top of as quickly as possible. He was big and broad, with hard muscles, tanned skin, and a confidence that couldn't be faked. His hair was almost a cross between dirty blond and brown, slightly mussed but somehow still sexy. Those blue eyes were startling though. Alert. She'd seem him looking her over, but when they'd touched, she'd been shocked at the electric current that zapped right through her.

When Luke's big hand had gripped her waist, she'd been all too aware of him, of the heat radiating off his big frame. A guy like that no doubt was used to getting what he wanted, to commanding the room. He'd literally laughed out loud when she'd said she wouldn't sleep with him. His friend seemed like a pig, what with flirting with the bartender all the while asking where he and his buddies could meet some other girls. She didn't know what to make of Luke though. He wasn't overly cocky, just self-assured. He'd held onto her a moment too long, making sure she was okay, and Wren could still feel his bulging biceps beneath her fingertips. The man was sexy as sin.

She shook her head, trying to clear her thoughts. She was here for her sister, not to meet a man. Showing Lily's photo to guests on the beach that afternoon had been a bust, and she'd realized all she was doing was drawing more attention to herself. The last thing she needed was word getting around that someone was here at the resort flashing photos of a teenaged girl.

Wren paused at the edge of the bar area, looking around as she tried to formulate a plan. She hadn't found YankeesE on the beach—not that she knew what he looked like. As she scanned the crowd, she was shocked to see Luke watching her from the bar, his gaze intense even from across the room. Luke's blue eyes held hers, but his face was stoic. Unreadable. He'd smelled faintly of aftershave and soap, something woodsy and male.

She felt herself flushing and quickly looked away. Wren didn't need a distraction, and remaining anywhere near him was just that. His muscular physique was appealing, but when he'd locked those eyes on hers? It was almost like all the air had been sucked out of the space around them. A man like him was dangerous. He might not hurt her physically, but falling into bed with a guy like that was still risky. She had no interest in getting burned.

"Hey, did you find your sister?" a man asked, snapping her focus back to the present.

Her gaze swung around to see a man with his family—his wife and elderly parents. It was an odd group to be in Cancun together, but she didn't think he was her guy. "Oh, um, yes, thanks."

"Good," he said, flashing her a quick smile.

She nodded at him but kept moving, looking around. She'd really hoped YankeesE would show up tonight, but what if he didn't? She'd spent all afternoon wandering around the beach and resort. The most recent picture he'd posted on social media had included part of his face, his eyes hidden behind a pair of Nike sunglasses. She'd barely noticed the logo with the way his head was turned, but there was just enough of it to make out. She could tell he was Caucasian, but that was it. Besides, no one would be wearing sunglasses tonight.

Wren was wasting time standing around here doing nothing. Her gaze tracked across the crowd again, focusing only on older men, fifties and up. One guy nearby was there was his wife, but she decided to go chat with them a moment anyway. "Hi! I'm a travel writer from New York. Do you both come to this resort often? I'm trying to find out from guests what makes it so popular."

"Fifth time here," the man said.

Wren's ears perked up. "Oh really? And why do you and your wife like coming here in particular?"

The two exchanged a glance, and he chuckled. "My wife's at home. We come here on vacation to have a good time." Wren's gaze darted between the two of them. Was this his…mistress? Gross. Either way, she wasn't a young teenager. If he was already sneaking around and leaving his wife at home, would he have time to bring teenage girls here to Mexico? It seemed unlikely.

The woman he was with answered Wren's question. "It's a beautiful resort. It's got great beaches and bars, and the spa is to die for. If you have time, get the hot-stone massage."

"Awesome. Thanks for the tip." Wren pulled out her phone, dictating notes to herself. Might as well play the part. "I'll be sure to check out the spa while I'm here," she said with a wink. "Thanks again." She spoke with a few other people but didn't learn anything useful. YankeesE had been at this exact bar though. The photos on his social media feed were proof of that. Where was he?

Realizing that Luke and his friends had left their barstools, she moved toward the female bartender. If they were actually looking for women, it stood to reason that they might like the same bars or nightclubs that YankeesE did. The disappointment she felt in that was surprising. Did they want to meet women to hook up for a night or were they looking to pay by the hour? Nausea roiled through her. Plenty of men would see nothing wrong with that, but it was also hard to imagine why they'd need to do that. Luke and his friends were young and fit. She imagined they had physical careers—athletic trainers, construction, firemen. She wasn't sure. Certainly, they wouldn't have trouble meeting women on vacation.

"Hi," Wren said to the woman tending bar as she slid onto an empty barstool. "You know those guys you were talking with earlier? Where did you recommend that they go tonight?"

"I told them about a few nightclubs in the area," the bartender said, wiping down the counter. "There are plenty of girls they could enjoy a good time with."

Wren bristled. "Oh yeah? Like tourists?"

The woman shrugged. "Yes and no. Can I get you a drink?"

"What do you mean by that?"

The woman studied her, licking her lips. "Tourists have money to spend, and the locals have to make a living. They'd be happy to see some American men and their fat wallets. As for any others? I can't say."

Wren frowned. "Right. What are the names of the nightclubs?" she pressed.

The crowd around them was growing louder, and she could sense the bartender already losing interest in the conversation. The woman named a couple of places, with Wren pulling them up on her phone. She wasn't too keen on the idea of venturing around Cancun herself, but what could she do? She'd come here looking for answers.

"Did they say where they were heading first?" Wren asked.

"Sorry, I'm not sure. If you don't want a drink, I need to take some orders."

Wren nodded and slid off the barstool, her sandals slapping on the ground and sundress swishing with the movement. Her gut instinct was telling her she should check out one of the clubs. Searching the hotel seemed pointless when she had no idea what room Lily may have been in or if she was still there. Besides, she could always do that during the daytime. Luke and his friends had left for more action, and maybe the asshole who'd kidnapped Lily had as well. She looked down at her phone, deciding to head to the closest place first. Ava was no doubt still on an airplane, but Wren texted her. In case anything happened, she needed to let someone know where she'd gone. Tomorrow they'd snoop around the resort and then head out together at night and cover more ground, but Wren couldn't waste any more time.

She clicked on Lily's social media account, staring at her sister's smiling face. There were no new pictures. No updates. Nothing. Wren bit her lip, fighting the tears that threatened to fall, and then hustled toward the concierge to get a taxi.

Chapter 7

"This place is a dump," Luke said, looking around the seedy nightclub. Waitresses walked around in skimpy clothes, drunk men groping at them, and the air was thick with the stale smell of cigarette smoke. The stage had seen better days, with one light busted, and the tables looked like they hadn't been wiped down in a week. The alcohol was flowing, however, with the crowd getting louder as music thumped over the speakers. It was off the main stretch of road but easy enough to get to. He wasn't worried about himself or his friends, but the other tourists who'd wandered in might be targets for theft or worse.

"Yep," Sam said, crossing his arms as he looked around. "No wonder our bartender suggested it. I was just talking to another local," he said, nodding toward a man nursing a beer. "There's a band playing soon, but the real entertainment comes after," he said in a low voice. "Women. And they're auctioned off for the night to the highest bidder."

"Holy shit," Ford muttered.

Sam's gaze swept toward a hallway in the back. "There're rooms back there. I want to check it out and see if the girls are being held. It could be local women here willingly, but if the trafficking ring operates out of this club…."

"It was on our list of targets," Luke said with a frown. "Juan Lopez's ring operates out of here. The bartender at the resort basically confirmed it by telling us where we could find women. I wonder if there's an after-hours event at the club Gray and Nick are searching."

"They'll have to stick around to find out," Sam said darkly. "If we don't get any leads tonight, we'll have to visit the others on the list tomorrow. Those girls are here somewhere."

"It kills me to be here in Cancun and not moving in," Luke said. "We knew the exact location of the kidnapped girl on our last op. Needing boots on the ground to gather intel is slowing everything down."

"I've got a feeling about this one," Sam said. "The locals know as much about the drug cartels and trafficking rings as the Bureau, and this place was mentioned by both the Feds and the bartender."

"You were really laying it on thick back at the resort," Ford said with a smirk.

Sam lifted a shoulder. "She slipped me her number, too. If nothing else pans out, I'll reach out. She might be helpful if we need additional information." His gaze swept the nightclub again.

Luke's phone buzzed, and he slid it from his pocket and glanced down at the text.

Jett: *West is working on the photo now. Good eye spotting*

his reflection.

Jett: *He'll have an image to you soon.*

Luke: *Thanks boss.*

"West is sending us a photo soon," Luke told the others. "At least that'll give us something to go off when searching the resort. Flying in blind isn't ideal."

"I'm going to scope out the back hallway," Sam said. "This is a large space, but given the satellite imagery we have of all the nightclubs, there's a lot more."

"There should be an exit to the alley back there," Ford said in a low voice. "West said he can get us detailed schematics if needed. He told me earlier that the nightclub's IT security was basically nonexistent. He can hack in and get the layout of any of the clubs. Once we know where the packages are, we can get blueprints of the building and determine the best way to exfil."

"Unless we buy them ourselves," Sam mused. "We pretend we're interested in the girls and then sneak them out."

Ford stiffened, looking angry. None of them liked the idea of buying girls for the night, even if they never intended to harm them. The women wouldn't know their purpose, however, and would no doubt be terrified.

"Let's see where we're at after tonight," Luke finally said. "If it comes to that, we'll do it. I'd like to get them out another way if possible, without drawing any attention to ourselves by bidding on girls. No doubt they track the customers, hoping for repeat clients and making sure everyone is who they say they are. They're running a business, as fucked up as it is." He glanced around, noticing that there didn't seem to be any other exit doors. "It looks like the only other way out of this club is the front. Guess they don't have the same fire code as in the States," he said, scrubbing a hand over his jaw. "If there were ever an emergency, it would be hell to get out of here."

"Then we'll hope that doesn't happen," Sam said. "Although if we need to extract multiple girls, it could be a problem."

"What if there are others?" Ford pressed. "We're aiming to rescue the three teenagers, but what about other women being held against their will?"

"We'll get them all to safety," Luke said, his fist clenching.

"And if the kidnapped teenagers aren't at any of the clubs?" Ford asked.

Luke's jaw twitched. "The ring operates out of the clubs. If they were sold to someone else, we'll find them. That would go against the usual way they traffic victims, however. In the long run, they make more money this way by allowing new men access to them every night."

"Fuck," Ford muttered. "That's so messed up."

Just then, a Mexican man walked quickly toward them, talking rapidly in Spanish as his eyes narrowed. His black hair was slicked back into a short ponytail, and tattoos covered his thick arms. He was shorter than the men on the Shadow Ops Team but didn't let their bigger size dissuade him from aggressively approaching. No doubt others were spread around the club watching them as well. "You American cops?" he asked in accented English, glaring at all three of the men.

"Nope," Sam said. "The bartender at our resort told us about this place. Said we could meet some girls here and have a good time."

"You better not be cops," he said.

Luke crossed his arms. "We were told this was the place to find some girls. Were we wrong?"

The man studied him for a moment then raised his hand, rubbing his thumb and forefinger together. "We own the police here in Cancun. There will be no trouble from you."

"Understood," Sam said, peeling several fifties from his wallet and handing them to the guy. "Just tell us where we can find some women. Our bartender promised us this place would be a good time."

"You want girls, huh?"

"Fuck yeah. Tell us where to get some pussy."

The man slid the money into his pocket. "You will wait like everyone else. Later tonight is the auction. Your money is good here as long as you don't cause any problems."

"Understood," Luke said, resisting the urge to grab the asshole and shake some more information out of him. The idea of auctioning off women was appalling. He had no idea if the missing teenagers would be among the ones they saw tonight—the women who were being sold. Either way, it made his stomach twist. They were supposed to be scouting out the place, but if Lily or her friends were here, he wasn't sure he'd be able to stop himself from rescuing them. Standing back and watching while they were hurt was unconscionable.

"Two hours," the man barked. "Then you can pay for a woman." He gave them the once over and then stormed off. Luke watched him raise his right hand in the air, signaling someone. The bouncers were easy to spot, but he knew there were other members of the human trafficking ring scattered around as well. He and his teammates had to be careful, because now they were on the club's radar.

As if they'd been summoned, a group of men came walking out from the back hall, hair slicked back and tattoos covering their arms. "Incoming, four o'clock," Luke said in a low voice. One of the men was adjusting himself in his pants, and Luke felt rage coursing through him. He had no idea if any of the women in the back were there of their own free will. What had those assholes been doing?

"Looks like our guy has some friends," Ford muttered in a low voice.

"They don't look too friendly," Sam commented dryly.

Luke turned away and spoke quietly into his mic, updating Nick and Gray.

"Roger that," Nick said. "We'll ask around, but I don't think there's any sort of auction here, just dancers who are happy to entertain clients in private. There are plenty of vacationers and lots of girls eager to take their money. None of the dancers are the missing teenagers."

"We'll stick around here for the auction tonight," Luke said. "In the meantime, we'll see if we can find out any info about an American man bringing women here. West should get us an image of this asshole soon. YankeesE works with these traffickers. He could be here right now."

Sam gestured that he was circling around and then strode off toward the men's room, near the back hall. The band playing seemed to be getting louder, the crowd pulsing with the music. Luke watched the people coming in through the front doors, many of them men. Tourists. A waitress slipped past, and he saw a man slap her ass. She startled for a moment then turned and blew him a kiss, clearly expected to play a certain role.

"Some of these guys look to be Americans, around fifty or so," Ford said. "Maybe one of them is him."

"Let's work the room," Luke said. "I want to see what we can find out. We've got some time to kill before they bring out the goods."

A new group of people were coming in through the front doors, and he stilled as he spotted a woman with long, dark hair in a gauzy sundress. She looked out of place at the nightclub, too pretty for the roughness and grime coating this club. As her head turned and deep brown eyes met his, he froze.

What the hell was a woman like Wren doing in a place like this?

Chapter 8

Wren's lips parted in surprise as Luke met her gaze. The nightclub was packed with people, and somehow the man who sent her pulse pounding had immediately noticed her. She swore she could still feel his muscular hand gripping her waist, his large body inches away. He was all beef and brawn, and something about his sure grip, steadying her, had made her feel simultaneously flustered but safe. She didn't know him, just had the sense that he wouldn't harm her. Luke's intense gaze was piercing, and his eyes narrowed, like he was annoyed she'd shown up here at the club. Well, too bad for him. She had just as much right to be here as anyone else. If he and his friends wanted to pay for female company or whatever it was they'd come for, then so be it. It's not like Wren would get in the way. She was here for one reason and one reason alone—her sister.

Luke leaned over, talking with his friend, and

Wren could tell even from across the room that he was letting his buddy know she was here. She didn't see the third guy from earlier, but no doubt he was around as well. Both men looked at her then, clearly unhappy at her arrival, and she turned away, her cheeks heating. Wren had no reason to feel embarrassed. Lots of other tourists were here. She swore she could still feel the intensity of Luke's gaze on her as she walked further into the club. Did he think she'd followed them? She had, in a sense. But she wasn't looking to chase after him.

Not that Luke knew that.

Her phone buzzed, and she realized that Ava had gotten her text. She was still in the air but must've paid for wi-fi.

Ava: *You're at a nightclub alone? Be careful!*

Ava: *You don't know how dangerous these men are.*

She clutched her phone, frustrated. Of course she knew how dangerous they were. They'd kidnapped Lily, hadn't they?

Wren: *I'll be careful. I just need answers.*

Just then, a guy around her age in a baseball jersey approached, asking if he could buy her a drink. His eyes were glassy, like he'd already had a few himself. "Sorry," she said breezily, "I'm meeting a friend."

"Aw, come on sweetheart," he said, reaching out as she stepped neatly to the side. "Don't be like that."

"No thanks," she said more firmly, moving away.

Her gaze swept the area. How in the hell was she supposed to find YankeesE in this crowd? She didn't even know what he looked like or if he was actually here. Her hunch could mean nothing. If the bartender had told Luke and his buddies to come here looking for women though, maybe she'd also suggested it to him. And maybe she'd find out something about Lily and her friends.

Uneasiness washed over her as she moved further into the club. Wren looked out of place in her sundress. While it had been fine for a beachfront resort, it didn't look right at a nightclub. The waitresses wore halter tops and short shorts and were teetering around in heels, carrying trays of drinks. Still, she could sense the male attention on her— interest that made her uncomfortable. She'd do anything to find Lily, but there were tons of nightclubs in Cancun. She might've come here tonight for nothing. A leering gaze at her cleavage had her turning away, but a conversation to her right piqued her interest. She paused and pulled out her phone, pretending to look at it as she listened.

"We were here last night, too," a man was loudly bragging to several guys over the thumping bass. He was gripping his beer, smiling as he talked about his conquest. "I had to come back for another round."

"That good, huh?" a short guy asked with a chuckle.

"Oh yeah. The chick I banged was hot as hell— tightest pussy I've ever had."

Wren stifled a gasp, trying not to draw attention to herself as she eavesdropped. Most of the men here were no doubt crude and obnoxious if they were coming for sex. There were plenty of women around, but the people who'd come to drink and dance were different than the groups that were coming for more nefarious purposes.

"They'll bring the girls out later," the guy continued. "You can take your pick as long as you fork over the dough up front," he added with a low chuckle. "The men running the place don't take kindly to anyone trying to lowball them. Be prepared to pay up, and you're golden."

She tucked that detail away, moving around them. Wren had no idea how they were finding or paying for the girls here. What did he mean they'd be out later? The waitresses were busy serving drinks, so she imagined there were more women somewhere else. And were they here by choice or by force?

Wren walked past several tables and booths, looking at the crowd on the dance floor. Everything seemed dingy and unclean. As she turned, she noticed a hallway in the back. Her heartrate sped up as she realized a man across the room was staring at her. Tattoos covered his muscled arms, and his dark hair was slicked back into a ponytail. He almost seemed to be guarding the back area, making sure no one went that way. She frowned, not liking that he was still watching her.

A group of women was standing near the bar, and she beelined toward them. The loud bass from the band onstage would make it hard to talk to anyone, but standing around alone wasn't a good idea, especially with that creepy guy watching her. Wren didn't need to draw any attention to herself.

She ordered a beer, deciding that was the safest bet. She could see the bartender popping the cap off, and he slid it across the bar to her. She laid some cash down, planning to mingle in a few minutes.

"Cute dress," one of the women near her said, looking over at Wren.

"Thanks. It might've been better for the beach, not a club, but oh well. This place is packed," she commented.

"It is. We decided to come out dancing tonight," a blonde woman said, taking a sip of her margarita. "Looks like we found one of the hotspots."

"The bartender at my resort recommended it," Wren told them.

"We haven't been to this club yet, but last night was fun." She rattled off the name of another local club, but it wasn't on the list the bartender had given Wren. Still, she tucked away the name in the back of her mind, just in case.

"I'll have to check it out. Was it nicer than this place? I heard some men talking about paying for women for the night here," she confided.

"Gross. I'm sure it happens at a bunch of these places," the blonde said with a frown. "The men probably have tiny dicks and can't get laid otherwise." One of her friends snorted, and Wren's lips quirked. While that may have been true, she didn't like thinking about the women being sold off for the night. Most of them probably weren't willing participants.

"I'll have to check it out another night. I'm not sure what to think of this place."

She looked around, noticing one of Luke's friends edging along the side of the nightclub toward the back hallway. The pony-tailed guy was gone, and she frowned. Were there really women back there? And what was Luke's friend doing? The guy's head swiveled left and right, and then he disappeared down the hall, moving swiftly for a man his size.

"I've got to find the ladies' room," she quickly told the other women.

Gripping her beer in one hand, she wove through the nightclub. Luke's friend hadn't reappeared, and rather than stop in the bathroom as she'd told the others, she slipped down the hall while no one was watching.

Wren was surprised to find it empty, and she continued moving further into it, wondering what exactly she was supposed to do now. She'd half expected someone to stop her. The thumping of music was getting quieter, and she slowed her steps as uneasiness washed over her. The area was dimly lit, and she counted at least five doors on each side. What the hell was this place?

She paused, hearing someone softly crying inside of the rooms. There was a muffled conversation and then a smacking sound. Her gaze landed on the doorknob, and then she froze when a man's voice began rapidly yelling in Spanish behind her. She looked up in surprise, taking a step back as the man hustled down the hallway, glaring at Wren. His eyes slid from the beer in her hand to her cleavage, and she swallowed, suddenly afraid.

"Sorry. Where's the bathroom?" she asked, pretending she was lost. "Is it in any of these rooms? I didn't see a sign."

The man continued talking loudly, gesturing for her to come with him. Wren's eyes darted around as she tried to decide if she needed to run. Would he let her move past him? Where did he want to take her?

"There you are!" a deep voice called out, and she wanted to cry in relief as Luke's friend suddenly appeared. He'd seemingly come out of thin air, but she'd known he was back here someplace. The guy towered above her, and he wrapped his arm around her shoulders, pulling her close as he nudged her forward. "She was looking for the bathroom," he said, guiding her away. "Sorry about that."

The Mexican man followed them, still angry, but didn't seem to want to take on Luke's muscular friend. She instinctively pressed closer to the guy who'd come to her rescue. Luke was waiting for them at the end of the hallway, his jaw clenched. He looked even bigger than earlier, his body tense, as if he was ready for a fight. His gaze flicked from her to the angry Mexican man behind them. She didn't say a word, just ducked into the ladies' room to keep up the charade, the rest of the nightclub still pulsing around her.

Wren heard the man who'd been yelling at her talking to both guys before the door swung shut. She shuddered as she closed the bathroom stall, setting the bottle of beer down. So far, she'd learned almost nothing but drawn plenty of attention to herself. It had been dumb to go back there alone, and she wouldn't be able to snoop around at all now. Who had been crying in the rooms though? Nothing good was happening here.

Grabbing her phone, she pulled up YankeesE profile on the app. Of course he hadn't posted anything since this afternoon. It would've been too easy if she knew exactly where he was right now. Taking the time to collect her thoughts and soothe her frazzled nerves, she was surprised to find both Luke and his friend waiting when she came out of the bathroom a few minutes later.

"Are you okay?" Luke asked, his eyes narrowing. Still, his blue gaze flicked over her, seemingly assessing that she was really all right. Heat coursed through her, both from his nearness and the careful way he was observing her.

"Yeah. I'm fine. Were you waiting for me?"

Luke didn't answer, but his friend stuck out his hand. "I'm Sam," he offered. She shook his hand, and while he was attractive in his own way, she didn't feel any of the electricity or sparks that she did when she and Luke had touched earlier. Even now, the air felt thick between them, charged. She could still smell his woodsy, masculine scent and feel the heat radiating off his big frame.

"Wren. And thanks for rescuing me back there."

"You shouldn't have been snooping around a place like this," Sam said, watching her carefully. "Are you here by yourself?"

"Why would I tell two men I don't know the answer to that?" she countered.

Luke looked irritated at her response, but Sam chuckled. "Fair enough. It's not safe to wander around here alone though. You're lucky I was back there."

"You were there alone."

Luke raised his eyebrows. "He's a lot bigger than you, sweetheart." She glared at him and couldn't quite place the expression on his face. He was worried, she realized. It was strange given they barely knew one another, but there it was. She'd met him all of once, so there was no need for him to feel protective of her. He seemed almost irritated that she'd been in danger.

"I just went the wrong way," she said, growing flustered. "And why were you back there anyway?" she asked, glancing at Sam. "Still looking to meet women, I presume?"

"Something like that," he murmured.

Wren watched in surprise as Luke lifted his hand to his ear. He was listening to something, she realized.

Startled, her gaze went from Luke to Sam. He was wearing a small earpiece as well. Both men were muscular and fit, and they practically oozed confidence from their pores. Were they police? Bodyguards? They didn't seem to be protecting anyone in particular, and she knew they didn't work here as security for the nightclub either.

"Are you guys cops?"

"No," Luke said, surprising her again with the intensity of his stare. "But we are investigating something. It seems like a coincidence that we met at the hotel and now here. Care to explain?"

"I'm looking for someone. I already told you that."

He nodded. "That you did. I'm not sure it's safe for you to be wandering around Cancun nightclubs by yourself though, Wren. The guys running this place—they're dangerous. The cops here are dirty. If you get yourself in trouble, there'll be no one to help."

Irritation roiled through her. "Thanks for the lecture, but I'll be fine."

He raised his eyebrows. "Will you? Because it didn't seem that way a few minutes ago. What would've happened if Sam wasn't already back there? Do you want to end up like the other women being held here?" She blinked, trying to come up with a response. He wasn't wrong, but she'd gotten distracted.

"I heard someone crying."

The two men exchanged a glance. "What were you back there looking for?" Sam asked.

Luke crossed his arms, and Wren tried to ignore the veins running over his muscled hands and forearms. Why she was so attracted to a gruff man like him, she wasn't sure. Luke was nothing like the men she usually dated—journalists, lawyers, and Wall Street types. He seemed slightly rough around the edges, unfazed by whatever was happening at the club, not to mention a touch bossy. He hadn't made a move to leave yet. He wanted answers, none of which he'd get from her.

A group of college-aged girls moved past them, giggling as they went into the bathroom, and Wren watched in confusion as Luke quickly palmed his phone, scrolling through something on the screen. He was looking at photos, she realized. Sam's gaze was darting between the two of them, like he'd already realized something she hadn't. She moved closer, and her jaw dropped open as she saw one of the pictures Luke was looking at.

"Why the hell do you have a picture of my sister on your phone?" she asked angrily.

Chapter 9

"Your sister?" Luke repeated, looking at Wren in surprise. Her jaw was slack with shock, her eyes wide, and her face slightly pale. She swayed on her feet, and Luke clamped onto her waist again to steady her. Both of her hands wrapped around his, staring at the phone he was still holding. Lily Martin's picture stared back at them, and he didn't miss the slight tremble in Wren's touch. Her hands were so damn soft, but he couldn't even appreciate the feel of her touch with the panic etched across her face.

His gaze tracked to Sam, who didn't look fazed in the slightest. "They've got the same eyes," Sam said in a low voice. "I just realized it myself. The same facial structure. High cheekbones. Full lips. I can't believe I didn't notice it earlier. Lily is Wren's sister."

"Son of a bitch," Luke muttered, the similarities obvious now. Lily was younger, with blonde hair and lots of makeup, but they did have the same physical attributes. He looked from the photo back to Wren again. He'd been so distracted by his attraction to her, he'd missed it. He squeezed her waist gently, making sure she was okay, and she took a deep breath. Then she brushed her hair back, hands trembling, as she took a step away from him.

"You still haven't answered my question," Wren said, her voice rising. He didn't miss the slight wobble to it, and his chest tightened. "Why do you have Lily's picture on your phone?"

Sam was speaking in a low voice into his mic, updating their team on the newest development. Nick's voice came over his earpiece. "Lily's sister is here in Cancun? What the fuck?"

"Roger that," Sam said. "She's at the same nightclub we are, and we saw her at the resort earlier as well. We'll find out what's going on."

Luke's teammates would have to continue to scope out the nightclub on their own, because he needed Wren to tell him everything she knew. How the hell had she ended up in Cancun? Did she realize Lily was here? It made no sense, and he wasn't letting Wren out of his sight until he found out how she'd learned where her sister was being held.

"We need to talk," he said quietly, "and we can't do it here. There are people watching us." Luke gripped her upper arm, gently steering her toward the front door. She didn't resist, just walked with him back through the nightclub, looking shocked. The heat from her bare skin burned into his fingers, but he ignored it. Tamped down his body's reaction to her. He loosened his grip, making sure that he wasn't hurting her. Wren was trembling, probably from both anger and fear. He was a lot bigger than her, with probably a hundred pounds on her much smaller frame. She didn't fight him though, just let him guide her out.

"I'll escort you back to your hotel," he said in a low voice, releasing her arm as she walked outside with him. "I'll explain what I can. Then I want to find out everything you know about how Lily ended up in Cancun."

She looked at him, worry etched across her entire face. "Are you here looking for my sister?"

He didn't answer right away, just ducked down so his lips were near her ear. Her floral scent made his cock twitch, but he ignored the sudden lust flaming through him. He was working. Just because Wren was a beautiful woman didn't mean he'd act on it. "Yes, but we'll talk about it back at the resort. I've got no idea who'll overhear us right now."

She bit her lip but nodded.

The music grew quieter behind them as the doors shut, and he gestured for a cab. Wren stepped slightly closer to him as a group of drunken men walked by. Unable to resist, he rested his hand lightly on the small of her back, guiding her away. "You're safe with me," he assured her. She looked up at him in surprise but nodded. She had no reason to trust him, but he liked that she felt comfortable enough to let him take her back to her hotel and protect her if necessary right now.

The group disappeared inside the nightclub, but she remained at his side. Why that felt so fucking right, he didn't want to examine too closely. He'd met Wren an hour ago and knew next-to-nothing about her. That didn't stop the waves of protectiveness that washed over him. She was frightened, whether she'd admit it or not. Luke felt the need to keep her safe and assure her she'd be okay.

A cab pulled up, and Luke opened the door, helping Wren into the back. His hand remained on her bare arm, and he immediately slid in beside her, forcing her to scoot over. She looked surprised for a beat but then seemed to realize he was doing it for her safety. The cab couldn't drive away while he walked around the car to the far door with Wren still inside. While Cancun wasn't traditionally a high-crime area as far as kidnapping tourists on vacation, he wasn't taking any chances with her safety, especially with her sister already missing. They'd already drawn some attention to themselves earlier, and he had no idea who might be watching them right now.

Luke gave the name of the resort to the cab driver, his gaze sweeping the busy street as the cab pulled away from the curb. Ford's voice crackled in his earpiece. "Sam and I are still inside scouting out the nightclub. Supposedly the women come out in two hours."

"Roger that," Gray said. "The women at this club seem to be mostly locals. We're going to ask around, see what else we can dig up."

Luke let out a breath he didn't realize he'd been holding. While his teammates would continue investigating the two clubs, he had the victim's sister at his side. This was a lead he'd never expected, but she'd clearly discovered something to have ended up in Cancun.

Wren was clutching onto her purse, clearly nervous, and Luke rested one large hand over her two smaller ones. He wasn't sure where the need to comfort her came from, only that she seemed out of her element and scared. He looked out the window instead of at her, ensuring they were heading the right direction. She settled beneath his touch, however, and a warmth he hadn't expected filled his chest. They were silent on the short drive back, but a few minutes later, he was helping her out of the cab and handing the driver some cash.

"Oh, I've got—" She started to unzip her purse.

"I got it," he replied, resting his hand on the small of her back and guiding her forward.

The cab pulled away, Luke's gaze following it. He clicked on his mic, updating his teammates. "We're back at the resort. I'll let you know if I find out any pertinent information. Over."

"Where's a good place for us to talk?" he asked in a low voice, trying to remain focused. Wren was staring at him, no doubt still surprised that he had Lily's picture on his phone. They paused outside of the main building at the resort, Wren barely coming up to his shoulder. Her sundress blew in the breeze, and she was so pretty it almost fucking hurt to look at her. Luke was surprised at the waves of possessiveness that washed over him right then. Wren wasn't his, but hell if he didn't want to soothe and protect her. The fear in her eyes made his chest clench.

"Maybe the beach?" she suggested. "The cabanas and huts have seating. The bar looks pretty crowded, and the restaurants will also be loud right now. I've got a room here, but…." She trailed off.

"It's all right. You don't know me, so we can talk somewhere quiet but still out in the open."

"Okay."

If he'd thought Wren would be upset by their

involvement, he was wrong. She'd seemed almost relieved after she realized they were looking for the missing teenagers. He met her dark eyes. "Did you come to Mexico alone looking for Lily?"

"Yeah. My parents and I had reported Lily's disappearance to the police over a week ago, but they thought she was a runaway. When I figured out who she'd been chatting with online and where he was, I hopped on a plane. I texted them and the police detective and just arrived today."

"Jesus," he muttered. "That was brave but also reckless. These men are extremely dangerous. Let's go sit and talk. You can fill me in on what you know." His hand landed on the small of her back again, and then he was guiding her forward. She shivered slightly but didn't pull away. Wren seemed affected by him, too. Luke had met attractive women on missions before but couldn't explain the strange pull he felt toward her. He stayed close to her side as they crossed the lobby, and then they were moving around the crowded bar they'd been in earlier, heading toward the more secluded beach.

Thatched huts stood empty on the sand, the cabanas off to the right folded down for the night. The ocean waves were soothing, a gentle breeze blowing off the water, but his senses were on high alert. This wasn't a romantic getaway with a woman. His gaze swept the deserted beach, but he didn't sense that anyone was out there. Luke guided her to a thatched hut in sight of the bar. They could hear the music and see people drinking and laughing in the distance, but they were alone.

Wren kicked off her sandals as she settled on a chair, clutching her hands together. He sank down beside her, leaning close so they could speak freely.

"Don't be nervous," he said quietly.

"My sister is missing. Of course, I'm nervous." The moonlight reflected in her dark eyes as she looked at him, and he sucked in a breath. This business. A mission. Nothing more than that.

"Why don't you tell me how you ended up in Cancun."

She shook her head, studying him. "I want to ask you some questions first."

"All right," he acquiesced, trying to make her feel more comfortable. She shifted, and his gaze briefly dropped to her cleavage. Her sundress hugged her curves in a way that made his blood heat. Wren was sexy without even trying, and something about her sitting barefoot beside him made her seem all the more vulnerable. He hated that she'd been prowling around the nightclub alone, looking for answers. While he was somewhat impressed at her gutsiness, he was frustrated that she'd put herself in jeopardy.

"You said back at the nightclub that you're not cops. Do you work for the government? Like federal agents or something?" Wren asked.

He cleared his throat. "We're all former military. I'm with a security firm now."

"A security firm? Someone hired you to find Lily? My parents didn't mention anything like that, and she's been missing for well over a week." She was watching him closely, clearly ready to doubt whatever he said.

Luke blew out a sigh, trying to decide what to tell her. He needed information, and he didn't think lying about his involvement would go over very well. Plus, she already knew that he had Lily's photo on his phone. "My friends and I work for Shadow Security," he said, going with the partial truth. "We provide protection to clients and work as bodyguards, typically for government or former government employees."

"That doesn't explain how you ended up looking for Lily," she pressed. "She's a teenager and certainly doesn't work for the government."

"We're former military, like I said, and sometimes we take on different tasks. Assignments. Your sister and her missing friends are about to be worldwide news."

"Oh shit," she whispered, pulling out her phone. She swiped the screen, her hands shaking. "I tried to hold off the news of Lily's kidnapping by calling in some favors. I knew it wouldn't last once her friends went missing as well."

"Why would you do that?" he asked sharply.

She slanted him a look. "Because if her face was everywhere they might kill her? I knew she didn't run away. Even before her friends disappeared, there was no way that was a possibility. She's a teenager in high school who loves her life. She's going to graduate next year and head off to college. She spent way too much time on social media, and my suspicions about that were correct. She trusted the wrong person and might live with the repercussions of that for the rest of her life." Wren let out a tiny moan of anguish as she scrolled through the news on her phone. "It's everywhere."

His gaze went from her phone back to her. "Once the additional teenagers went missing, it was inevitable."

"That's why you're here," she said astutely. "To

get them before it's too late."

"It is. We were tasked by the government to come and find them. What do you mean that you called in a few favors?" Luke asked.

"I'm a journalist. One teenage girl missing wasn't going to be national news, but it might've been local and gotten blown up. You never know what stories the media will hone in on. I wanted to protect her. Believe me, I had my doubts. Would her face blasted everywhere hurt or help?" She shrugged helplessly. "I thought I was doing the right thing to keep it out of the media."

"Did your family go to the police when your sister disappeared?"

"Of course we did," she said, looking annoyed. "They didn't believe us or want to do a damn thing about it. They considered her a runaway. I spent all week trying to get into Lily's social media accounts. I could see all the pictures she'd posted and comments but knew she had to be messaging someone privately."

"You hacked into her account." It wasn't a question.

Wren swiped the screen on her phone again. "I got locked out of one account but managed to get into another. She was messaging a lot of different men."

"Fuck," he swore quietly.

"But I found that man that she met."

Surprise washed over him. "You found him?"

She shot him another look. "I'm here, aren't I? She was communicating with this guy, YankeesE." Wren held up her phone, and Luke was staring at the same social media profile he'd been monitoring. "I got into her account though, so I could see the private messages between them. He picked her up from my parents' house. She snuck out, and that was that. She's gone."

"Son of a bitch," he muttered. "And how did you know to come to Mexico? Did the messages say that?"

She shook her head. "I stumbled upon that accidentally. He's been posting a lot of pictures himself. I figured out the name of the hotel from doing a reverse image search." Luke's ears perked up. She was sharp. Foolish, maybe, to rush down on her own, but smart.

"That's how we determined his location as well," Luke said.

"Lily's here, too," she told him. "Or she was."

His gaze narrowed. "We suspect he brought her to Mexico, but what led you to believe that?" he asked, curious.

Wren swallowed, looking upset again. She fumbled with her phone. "Look at this picture," she said, turning the screen toward him again. Luke glanced down at the photo of a bottle of beer. "See that?" she said, pointing to the hand resting on the bar, off to the side. "The tattoo."

"Is that a flower?" he asked, looking more closely at the piece that was visible in the photograph.

"It's a lily."

Realization washed over him. "Jesus," he said, thoughts turning over in his mind. "We didn't have any evidence that she'd been at this hotel until now. We were searching for her kidnapper. I'll have our IT guys review all the surveillance footage at the resort from over the past week. They can run her image first. If this guy was with Lily, we can use facial recognition software to determine his identity. We can get his room number and ascertain if she's still being held here, although it's most likely that she's been moved at this point."

Luke spoke into his mic, updating his teammates.

"Shit, man," Gray muttered over his earpiece. "If she was in the hotel days ago, I doubt she's still there now."

"Agreed, but we can search the room and get a photo of the man she's with. Facial recognition software might even give us a name."

"His time as a free man is numbered," Sam seethed.

Wren was staring at the photo showing Lily's tattoo, her eyes watery. Luke felt the sudden need to comfort her, even though they didn't know much of anything at this point. "We don't know what's happened," he said in a low voice. "They could've moved her to another location, waiting for whatever is planned."

"She could be hurt," Wren said, swiping at the tears that started rolling down her cheeks.

"I'm sorry," he murmured. "Can I see the messages she was exchanging with him?"

Wren looked surprised for a moment but then nodded. "Of course. Like I mentioned, she was chatting with a bunch of men. This was the one she gave my parents' address to."

"They're in Philadelphia," he said, taking the phone from her. Their fingers brushed, and he tried not to react at the feel of her smooth skin against his own calloused hands or listen to the slight hitch of her breath. "Is that where you live?"

She shook her head. "I'm in New York City."

"Our headquarters is north of there," he commented. Why he felt the need to share that information, he wasn't sure. It didn't pertain to the case, but for some reason, he liked knowing she lived relatively close. It was a big damn world, after all. What were the chances he'd meet an attractive woman that lived an hour away from him? Next to nothing.

"What were you guys doing at the nightclub?" she asked. "Do you think this guy, YankeesE, was there?"

"If not tonight, I'm sure he has been." Luke explained his connection to the human traffickers and the list of nightclubs, telling her about the auction they'd discovered. Wren grew paler and paler the longer he spoke.

"We have to go find her," Wren said urgently, standing up. She fumbled with her sandals, slipping them back on. "We need to go back there. I can't let them sell my sister for a night. I can't," she repeated, panicking.

"Wren," he said, rising himself. Luke towered over her and reached out, his large hand lightly gripping her arm. "Sam and Ford are there. If Lily is among the women being auctioned off, they'll get her. The best thing we can do right now is compare notes. There's no guarantee Lily is one of the women at that particular nightclub. My buddies are already checking out another club in Cancun that also has ties to a sex-trafficking ring. There are multiple places we need to search. Our goal tonight is to gather information. We don't know where she's being held yet."

Wren swayed on her feet, and Luke muttered a curse, pulling her close. Her small hands landed on his chest, and she blinked away her tears as she clung to him.

"It's all right," he said soothingly. "We'll find her. I swear to you I'm not leaving Mexico without your sister."

"Me either," she said softly, still clutching onto Luke.

He met her worried gaze. "Have you eaten anything since you arrived in Mexico? You look really pale."

"No," she said weakly. "I had a few sips of a margarita earlier at the hotel bar. That was hours ago."

Luke frowned. "You probably have low blood sugar, and I'm sure you've been stressed out and not sleeping well given your sister's disappearance. Let's grab something to eat so you don't pass out on me, and then you can tell me more about what you've discovered. I barely glanced at the messages your sister exchanged with that asshole, and it's possible we can get more clues from that exchange. Let's go over it together."

"Okay. I guess I can eat. I want to know more about your team as well."

"Then let's grab some food," he said, nodding toward the resort. "And then I'll bring you up to speed on what we know so far."

Chapter 10

Wren awoke with a start the next morning, gasping for breath. She was twisting in her sheets, fighting against nothing, her short, strappy nightgown clinging to her skin. She finally kicked off the covers, pressing her hand to her chest as her heart raced. What had woken her? Grabbing her cell phone from the nightstand, she looked to see if Luke had texted her any updates. There was nothing but the text Ava had sent in the middle of the night, which she'd already seen. Ava's flight had been diverted to Dallas because of bad weather, and she was supposed to land in Cancun later this morning.

Wren let out a sigh. She was hoping to see a call or text from Luke saying that they'd found her sister. She'd talked with Luke for nearly two hours last night, poring over the messages Lily had exchanged with various men. Luke had grown furious at YankeesE for goading Lily into sending him partially nude photos. He'd told Wren that the guy was believed to be a Marine officer. It made sense given what the bartender had said about the man with Lily being in great shape, but it was also sickening that a man who should be serving his country was harming the very people he'd sworn to protect.

Luke had made some notes and asked if she could text him screenshots of all the messages. After he'd passed the info on to his boss at Shadow Security, she'd even let Luke walk her back to her hotel room. It had been late, and maybe she'd put too much trust in a man she didn't know, but she felt safe with him.

Her phone buzzed just then, and she jolted in surprise, staring down at the text.

Luke: *Good morning. The guys said she wasn't spotted at either club last night.*

Luke: *They got back late, and I didn't want to wake you.*

Wren bit her lip, hating the tears that filled her eyes. She'd assumed as much given that she hadn't heard from him. If it was urgent, she knew he'd have called. She stood up, adjusting her nightgown. It hugged her breasts and curves, hitting at mid-thigh. She ran a hand through her hair, wondering if she looked as bad as she felt. It had taken forever to fall asleep, and it hadn't been restful in the least. She thumbed a quick response to Luke.

Wren: *Thanks. Let me know if you find out anything.*

Luke: *Will do. Sorry if I woke you.*

Wren: *No worries. I didn't sleep well and was already up.*

She set her phone back down, wondering why she'd even texted him that. Luke wasn't her boyfriend, just a man she'd spent several hours with the night before, who'd been tasked to find her sister. Luke was here in Mexico for a job. If she found him attractive, so be it. It's not like anything had happened or ever would. At the moment, she needed to shower, get dressed, and meet with Ava soon. There was no need to think about the muscular guy with piercing blue eyes who made her feel protected when he was near.

The tiny coffee maker in her room looked like it couldn't produce a decent cup of anything, and Wren tried to decide if she should order room service or go grab a coffee herself at the little café downstairs. She crossed to her suitcase, wondering what to wear. She'd tossed things in quickly in her haste to leave New York but had managed to bring a decent selection. A knock on her hotel door a minute later had her frowning, and as she hurried over and looked through the peephole, she let out a squeak of surprise. Luke was standing there looking better than any man had a right to at that early hour, freshly showered, with damp hair and clean clothes. Luke's lips quirked as he clearly heard her cry of surprise, and her jaw dropped in shock at the two cups of coffee he was holding.

"Just a sec!" she said, frantically rushing back across the room to grab her satin robe. It was floral and would keep her covered, but it still wasn't entirely what she'd have chosen to wear the next time she saw Luke. She ran her hands through her hair again, looking down to make sure she was completely covered. As she opened the door, she realized she wasn't wearing any panties. Of course she wasn't. She was in her nightgown. Wren could already feel herself flushing. It wasn't like her to act that way around a man, but something about him had all her senses on high alert.

"Good morning," he said as the door swung completely open. His voice sounded deeper this early, gruffer somehow, and shivers raced down her spine. Wren was sure her cheeks were pink. He smiled and kept his eyes on her face, sensing that she was embarrassed. She didn't miss the hint of amusement in his own, however.

"Hi. I wasn't expecting anyone."

"I know. Sorry. I was at your resort looking around, getting a better feel of the entire layout, and thought I'd bring you a coffee. I grabbed one myself, so…." He shrugged. "I figured you could use it since you said you didn't sleep well."

"Thank you," she said, taking it from him in surprise. Luke showing up with coffee was about the last thing she'd expected. If her sister herself had appeared, Wren didn't think she'd be more shocked.

Luke was big and broad, taking up too much of her doorway. He held the door open with his big body, but she didn't feel crowded or unsafe. Her mind was still processing the fact that he'd shown up on her doorstep, so to speak. "I'm meeting with my teammates soon," he explained. "Our IT guy has a photo to send us that I'm interested to see. We were waiting on some enhancements."

"Oh yeah?"

"It's nothing great, according to him, but it's a picture of the man your sister was communicating with. There was a reflection in his sunglasses that we're working off."

"The Nike ones?" she asked. Luke quirked his brow. "There was a logo visible," she explained. She looked down at the coffee in her hand and then up at him. He wasn't about to invite himself in, but she could tell he was curious.

"Why don't you come in for a few minutes," she found herself saying. "I'll grab my phone and show you. I mean, if you want," she hedged.

"Sure thing, if that's okay. I want you to be comfortable. I meant what I said yesterday. You're safe with me."

She met his gaze, sensing the sincerity there, and nodded, inviting him in. He could've hurt her last night if he wanted. Wren had no reason not to trust him right now. She took a sip of the coffee as they walked into her hotel room, the door shutting behind Luke. "This coffee is fantastic. I love dark roast, and I desperately needed the caffeine. I was debating ordering room service so I didn't have to go out."

"Good," he said with a low chuckle. "As I was heading to your room, I realized I should've grabbed sugar and creamer. Then I worried the whole thing was a bad idea, but I knew you were up since you'd texted me back."

"I was. We'll just pretend I'm not standing here in my robe."

Luke snorted. "Whatever you say."

She did a double-take, and he lifted his shoulder, his lips quirking. "It's hard to forget a beautiful woman. I'll try though," he added with a wink. Flushing, Wren moved toward the small table in her room, picking up the sundress she'd discarded yesterday. Was Luke flirting with her?

Her face turned even redder as she snatched the skimpy thong from where it had fallen on the floor. Luke pressed his lips together, amused, but didn't comment. She shoved the clothes into her suitcase, quickly looking around to make sure she hadn't left any other undergarments lying around. Like she really needed him to see her lacy bras or other panties. They were working together to find her sister. Something about Luke just threw her off-kilter.

"Sorry, I'm a little frazzled today," she said. She glanced over at him, blinking in surprise at the way he was watching her. She couldn't interpret the look in those blue eyes. Concern, perhaps, but also something softer. Butterflies unexpectedly filled her stomach.

"You've got a lot going on," he said diplomatically.

"I can't believe I even flew down here. Nothing about this seems real." She bit her lip, frowning as she set her coffee down on the small table. A tinge of embarrassment still coursed through her, combined with a hint of arousal. Try as she might to pretend she wasn't standing here nearly naked in a robe, she was. And she was all too aware of Luke at her side.

"My parents texted me late last night," she said, trying to get her mind back on track. "They hadn't been checking their messages, which is weird. I guess the media stories shocked and upset them, so they set their phones aside for hours. They were furious that I flew down to Cancun."

"Are you close?"

"Close enough. I don't live nearby or anything, and Lily is ten years younger than me. The police detective finally responded as well. He wanted the messages she'd exchanged, just like you. I sent them along but am not too hopeful. I mean, you guys are here in Mexico. What can a police detective in Philly do?"

"Not much," Luke agreed. "The case already went to the FBI. My boss has contacts at the Bureau, which is how we ended up on this op."

Wren swiped the screen on her phone, swallowing. The way she reacted to him was crazy. She barely even knew they guy. Luke shifted, reaching over to grab a picture of her sister on the table, and she saw the weapon he carried. Of course, he had a gun. Hadn't he said he worked for a security firm?

Luke's gaze followed hers. "I wasn't carrying a weapon last night. The nightclub has metal detectors," he explained.

"Right. And you're former military."

"Delta Force," he said quietly.

"What's that? Like a Navy SEAL?"

He chuckled. "Like a SEAL but better," he said with a twinkle in his blue eyes. "We were sent on all types of missions—hostage rescues, taking out terrorists. Our team deployed all over the world."

"You seem young," she commented. "What made you get out of the military?"

"I'm thirty-four," he said with a laugh. "Not too young compared to the newly-enlisted guys. We had a mission go bad," he explained. "One of my teammates was taken hostage. Jett, our team leader, ended up starting Shadow Security. He brought us all on board to work for him."

She studied him. "You guys aren't just bodyguards."

He shook his head. There was clearly more he wasn't telling her, but Luke hadn't denied it. Taking on special jobs was one thing, but busting up a human-trafficking ring? Rescuing three kidnapped teenagers who'd been taken to Mexico? Luke and his friends were dangerous. They wouldn't hurt her, but for the first time, she felt a strange sense of calm. They were trained operatives who'd get Lily back. She didn't doubt it.

Wren pulled up the app on her phone, showing him the picture.

"You've got a good eye for detail," Luke said, studying it. He took a sip of his own coffee, and she noticed the way his Adam's apple bobbed. He'd shaved, so she could clearly see his chiseled jaw and masculine features. His big hand held the small paper cup, the veins evident under his skin, and for a flash, she imagined those hands trailing over her bare skin. He had thick fingers, and she wondered what it would feel like as he undressed her, caressing her curves as he untied her robe. Touched her intimately while she squirmed. Would he kiss her gently or be a demanding lover?

It was a crazy thought. Wren didn't sleep with strange men. She'd had her fair share of boyfriends over the years, but she'd always been in a committed relationship when she was intimate with a man. Luke had her mind spinning in circles. He looked calm and capable, and she was a flushed and frazzled mess.

Wren looked back at the photo on her phone, still feeling slightly dazed. "I guess my attention to detail is how I ended up in Cancun," she said with a shrug. "I figured out the hotel name from his photos. It seems dumb for him to post so much, doesn't it? I mean, I'm certainly no criminal mastermind, but I swear it's like he wants to be caught. I've investigated local politicians who were harder to track down. Why would a Marine officer post this online? It's almost like he wants people to know where he is."

"It's unusual and not what he's previously shared on the app. It's a game to him. Clearly, he knew how to play the part and find his victims. We're not sure what his endgame is. Although my team has been tasked to find your sister and her friends, we're hoping to bring this asshole down as well. Our IT staff at Shadow Security is already combing through the past week's surveillance footage at the resort."

"How did they get access?" she asked.

"They're the best at what they do. We didn't know what YankeesE looked like, but now that you've confirmed your sister was here, we can run facial recognition software looking for her on the resort cameras. I'll admit we were working under the scenario that she was taken to another location. It's not unheard of to traffic victims out of a hotel, but with this particular trafficking ring, they tend to work out of businesses they own—nightclubs and the like. No one expected for her to be here at all."

"Do you think she's still here?"

"It's unlikely. He brought her here for whatever dark purposes he had but most likely has already sold her to the traffickers."

"Shit," she muttered.

"I'm sorry," he said, his voice gentling. "If we find her on surveillance footage, we'll get him. Once we match his face to a name, it's over."

"For him at least," she murmured. "Lily is still missing. Oh, they were at the bar Friday," she suddenly remembered.

"Oh yeah?" Luke asked, raising his eyebrows.

"When I arrived yesterday, I showed a few people her picture, including the bartender. I just pretended I was meeting Lily at the bar but couldn't find her anywhere. The bartender said he'd seen her Friday night with my dad—obviously it wasn't my dad, of course. But he was positive she was there with a man."

"It was him," Luke said, clenching his fist. "YankeesE. Let me call my guys at headquarters. Having a specific time and location to review surveillance footage will help immensely. We'll get a shot of him and hopefully can ID the bastard. We're searching the place blind now, hoping to gather information."

Luke lifted his phone to his ear, and Wren looked around the hotel room, feeling silly that she was still in her robe. She rifled through her suitcase, grabbing some clothes. "I'll just—" She cocked her head toward the bathroom, and Luke nodded. He looked to the table and back at her. "Go ahead, sit down," she mouthed. He pulled out the chair and folding his large body into it, speaking in a hushed tone. Crossing toward the bathroom, she left Luke sitting there. She could hear his deep voice as she closed the door, awareness skittering over her. She paused for a moment as she locked it but instinctively knew she was safe. Luke wouldn't try to barge in here or hurt her. Wren could still hear him speaking into the phone.

She flipped on the fan and started the shower, trying to forget about the muscular man she'd left mere feet away. They'd get a lead and find this guy. Rescue Lily. Luke would go back to his other jobs. She'd go back to the city.

Finding her sister was her only priority, but she felt the tiniest hint of remorse that she and Luke would part ways when this was over.

Chapter 11

Luke crossed the resort, heading to meet with his teammates. He'd stayed in Wren's room for an hour that morning, ending up on a conference call with Jett and West. Wren had come out of the bathroom with damp hair, looking so pretty, it made his chest hurt. She'd been barefoot, wearing shorts and a tank top, but her clothes hugged her sexy curves. Something about the floral scent of her soap or shampoo and everything else that was pure Wren made his pulse pound.

He'd been a perfect gentleman, not wanting to frighten her, but that hadn't stopped his libido from rising. It had felt intimate to be working together from her hotel room, their arms brushing as they worked at the small table, the chemistry between them undeniable. Things had remained strictly business, however. He'd filled Jett in on the call, and Luke could tell even his boss was impressed with the clues she'd uncovered. He'd left her to finish getting ready but hadn't missed the way her breath hitched as they'd said goodbye at her door. Luke had towered above her, unable to resist brushing a strand of hair back from her face. He had no right to touch her but couldn't help himself. Wren was smart and sexy but also sweet as hell. Her flushes around him were intriguing, not that he had time right now to explore anything between them.

"Hey man," Sam said, fist-bumping Luke as he walked up. Luke's mind immediately snapped back to the present. "Jett said he talked to you when you were inside Wren's hotel room?" He chuckled, looking amused, a smirk on his lips.

"Nothing happened," Luke said, refusing to let his buddy bait him. "I brought her a coffee since I knew she was up. We'd been texting."

"Texting before eight a.m.?" Nick asked, raising his eyebrows. "That's true love right there."

Luke lifted a shoulder. Spending time with her hadn't been a hardship in the least. "I knew she'd be worried about her sister. Last night was a bust, but I wanted to fill her in. She's devastated that Lily was taken."

The men sobered quickly at the reminder and headed to a quiet area of one of the restaurants to discuss strategy. With the morning breakfast rush over, most vacationers were on the beach or at the resort pool, which gave them a modicum of privacy here. The men grabbed chairs and sank down into them, pulling out their phones to go over information.

"West sent the image he enhanced from the reflection in the sunglasses," Luke said, looking at his phone. "It's not a great photo, but at least we have something to go off. Anything is better than nothing."

"Huh. I'd say he's around fifty. Buzz-cut like we expected," Ford said, looking at his own email from their IT guru.

Luke studied the image. "Wren pointed out that he had Nike sunglasses. You can see the little swoosh in the photo. We can spread out and canvas the resort today, see if we can find someone who looks like this guy."

"Fuck yeah," Nick agreed. "Let's find this mofo."

"Anyone heard from Gray?" Luke asked.

"He's checking out a bar he heard about last night. It wasn't on the list of nightclubs we got from the Feds, but we've got to do our due diligence. He heard they had some women available there and went to investigate."

"Shit," Luke muttered. "It's never ending with this group. We'll divide and conquer tonight, checking more of the clubs off our list. I'm also wondering about Juan Lopez. He's the ringleader but wasn't one of the men we saw last night. I sent photos of that ponytailed guy to West. Maybe he can ID him. I didn't recognize him from the dossier we were given."

"No doubt he's part of it all," Ford said. "He was guarding the back hallway for most of the night."

"Except for when Luke's girl snuck in," Sam said with a smirk.

"She's not my girl," Luke muttered.

"She's gutsy," Sam said in an admiring tone. "It was stupid, no doubt, but the fact that she even showed up in Cancun was surprising. It's a good thing you got her out of there before the auction."

"Hell," Ford said, scrubbing a hand over his jaw. "Watching those women getting sold for the night fucking burned me up. It wasn't Lily or her friends, but some of those girls were young. You know they weren't there by choice. They looked terrified."

"American?" Luke asked.

"I think they were all locals, supposedly there willingly."

"Which they fucking weren't," Luke ground out. "Jesus. I wish we could help all of those women. If we round up YankeesE, we'll learn more intel about Juan. I'd love to end that entire goddamn trafficking ring."

"Where's Wren now?" Sam asked, glancing over at Luke.

"She's meeting a friend," he explained.

Sam raised his eyebrows. "A friend who's in Cancun?"

"Yep," Luke continued. "She texted her best friend yesterday, who jumped on an airplane to come down and help look for Lily. Ava's supposed to be here soon."

"Ava?" Sam asked, a smirk on his lips. "Huh. I haven't heard that name in a while. I met an Ava once."

Nick chuckled. "Shit. That girl you met in Paris?"

"The very one," Sam said with a smile. "She was a firecracker—some artist or something. Not gonna lie—she was scorching in bed. Ava ordered champagne, strawberries, and chocolate sauce at the fancy hotel she was staying at. That girl painted me with the chocolate and then licked off every drop."

"Jesus," Nick said with a laugh. "Why don't I ever meet the wild chicks?"

"They're out there," Luke assured him. "You're just not looking hard enough."

"She was something else," Sam remembered. "I said goodbye to her the next morning, and that was that. She gave me her number but was backpacking around Europe, and we were on a layover and heading to another op. Never called her. I never forgot that night though."

Luke's phone buzzed, and he lifted it to his ear, putting his friend's one-night-stand out of his mind. Nights like that were long behind him. He hadn't even been with a woman in over six months. Hell. Wren in that silky little robe this morning would be hard to forget. He shouldn't have touched her as he'd said goodbye, but damn. The woman was irresistible.

"West," he said into the phone. "We just got the photo. You have anything else to go off? This is a good start but doesn't give us too many details on his appearance."

"I know. The reflection wasn't great in those sunglasses, even running it through my programs to enhance it. I've got good news though. We've been going through the surveillance footage and think we have a profile shot of this guy."

"No kidding?" Luke asked. "I'm putting you on speaker. The rest of the team is here."

Luke set the phone on the table, and the team listened as West filled them in. A moment later, they all received the email containing a still shot of YankeesE. "We're running this through several programs to see if we can get an ID on the guy. He was looking away from the camera at the bar, either coincidentally or not. A profile shot is better than nothing though. It might be enough to get a match in our systems. Once we have a name, it's over for him."

"Son of a bitch," Luke said, studying the profile picture. "This is good. We can see the entire side of his face. He's got a lot of gray hair mixed in with the dark. You can't tell as much with the buzz cut, but the stubble on his beard sure the hell shows it. It looks like his nose is slightly crooked, like it was broken at some point. And in the other photo, we could tell he has a broad forehead. Nike sunglasses."

"The crooked nose should make it easier to ID the guy. I'm certain we can find more footage of him at the resort, but I wanted to get this over to you ASAP so you can be on the lookout. I'll let you know as soon as I have a positive identification. Jett's here at headquarters with me and the IT staff. We'll get a name and end this."

"Appreciate it," Luke said. He eyed the rest of his teammates as he ended the call. "We should spread out and look for him. Chances are he's still here. Even if this asshole likes the nightclubs, it's early. He was still posting on that social media app yesterday. He spends his days here at the hotel."

"Did he post any new pictures today?" Nick asked.

"Nope, but it's early. I'll keep checking. I know Wren was monitoring it as well."

"She's sharp," Nick said, his head swiveling toward Luke. "Hope she stays out of trouble."

"Me too," Luke muttered. "I told her to let us handle the investigation, but she's a grown woman. There's not much I can do if she insists on joining in on searching for Lily."

"Tie her to the bed," Sam said, waggling his eyebrows. Luke shot him a look. "What?" Sam joked. "She didn't look too disappointed to be leaving the club with you last night."

"Nothing happened, jackass. We're working together to find her sister. That's all."

"Uh-huh. Keep telling yourself that."

Luke muttered a curse as the team stood up, filing out of the empty restaurant and into the hotel lobby. "I'm going to check with the bartender first," Luke said. "I'll show him the picture and see what he can tell me. Maybe he'll recognize YankeesE and can tell us a name or room number."

Ford's gaze scanned the lobby. "He's here somewhere. The photo yesterday was from late afternoon."

"We'll split up so as not to draw attention to ourselves," Luke said. "If he's waiting on something to happen, there's no need for us to tip him off."

A swish of long, dark hair caught his attention, and then he saw Wren rushing across the lobby and hugging a strawberry blonde woman who'd just come inside. Her friend had on a long, flowy dress and sandals, and was pulling a small hot pink suitcase behind her. They talked animatedly a moment, hugging again, and then the two women turned as the men walked in. Luke had no doubt they were an imposing force in the lobby—part of the reason they needed to disperse. A team of former Deltas wasn't exactly inconspicuous.

The new woman's mouth parted in surprise as she looked past Luke, and he heard one of his teammates muttering behind him.

"What in the world?" she asked quietly, looking shocked. "What are you doing here?"

"Motherfucker," Sam ground out. "Ava."

Chapter 12

Wren looked between Ava and Sam in confusion, taking in the expressions on both of their faces. Her normally outgoing friend was speechless, now looking slightly pale. "You know him?" Wren asked. Luke was talking quietly to Sam, who looked like he'd seen a ghost.

"Hell yes, I know him," Ava said. "He's the guy I spent a night with in Paris."

"The guy—oh." Wren's head spun as she remembered Ava gushing over the guy she'd met a year ago. The man she'd given her number to and who'd subsequently never called. Ava wasn't one to date seriously, preferring to have short-lived fun, but something about this had been different. As Wren recalled, Ava had spent the entire day—and night—with a handsome American soldier. She'd given him her number, made him promise to call her, and then she'd never heard from him again. She'd been heartbroken. Despite them barely spending twenty-four hours together, Ava had declared that they clicked in a way that was indescribable. It was kismet. Fate. And she'd never forgiven him for disappearing without so much as an explanation.

"Is she okay?" Luke asked, looking concerned. His gaze darted between Wren and Ava. Wren didn't miss the way Sam had frozen behind him.

"I'm fine," Ava said tightly. "I was just surprised to see your asshole friend."

"Ava," Sam hedged, reaching out.

"Too little, too late," she muttered. "If you didn't want to ever see me again, that would've been fine. But lying about it? Promising you'd call and then ghosting me? Give me a break. Why don't we go drop off my suitcase," she said, starting to walk away. "You can fill me in on your sister. I don't need to waste another second thinking about this jerk."

"Wait," Wren said, stopping her. "I know you're still mad at Sam, but these guys are actually here looking for Lily. All of them," she clarified.

Ava stilled, looking even more irritated. "So you really are in the military?"

"Former," he said, his gaze not leaving her face.

Ava shrugged, looking distraught. "Whatever. You're still a dick." She looked back to Wren as some of the other men chuckled. "Can we go to your room now?"

"Sure. I'll explain everything and what I know about Lily there," Wren said gently. "Just know that these guys are helping us."

"I actually wanted to speak with you a minute," Luke said, moving forward. He stopped beside Wren, not missing the way her friend was now glaring at him.

"You're friends with Sam?" Ava asked him.

"We're teammates," Luke explained.

"Great," she said sarcastically. Luke turned, gesturing for his friends to leave, and the men dispersed, Sam moving more slowly than the others.

"This is Luke," Wren said.

"Ava," she said, crossing her arms. Clearly, she wasn't about to shake the guy's hand. He nodded at her instead, not seeming offended.

"I've got a new photo to show you," Luke told Wren, his gaze serious. "It's from the surveillance footage. Our IT guys just sent it over."

"Oh," she said, surprise washing over her. "Can I see it?"

"Absolutely. Let's go someplace else though. I'll walk you to your room," he said, reaching for Ava's suitcase. She shot him a withering look, and Wren didn't miss the way Luke's lips quirked. "I promise I'll just be a minute," he assured her, grabbing the suitcase and guiding them to the elevators. "I want to show Wren this photo. She'll want a copy of it, too. We're looking for the same guy."

"Wait, how does he know where your room is?" Ava asked, still bristling.

"We had coffee this morning," Luke said smoothly, pressing the button.

Ava's jaw dropped as Wren rolled her eyes. "He texted me with an update earlier and then came by," she said, shooting him a look of annoyance. "It's nothing."

"Sorry," he mouthed, not actually looking sorry in the least. Wren tried not to smile. Ava's irritation toward him was kind of funny. Just because Sam had been a jerk didn't mean Luke was. At any rate, they were helping one another out. She wasn't about to have some crazy night of wild sex with the guy or fall in love with the man. They'd find her sister and go back to their own lives.

The elevator doors dinged, and they stepped inside, Luke pushing the number for Wren's floor. His big hand gripped the handle of Ava's luggage, and Wren noticed he didn't even bother setting it down. He was big and buff, towering above them in the elevator. Once again, however, his presence just made her feel safe.

"What kind of picture do you have to show us?" Ava asked. "Did you spot Lily somewhere?"

"No, but we finally got an image of the man she's with. Our IT guy just sent it to us a little while ago. It's a still shot from the hotel surveillance footage. Hopefully we can ID him from it."

"Seriously?" Ava asked, looking astonished.

Luke nodded, and the trio stepped off the elevator, moving down the hall. "The rest of the guys are searching the resort. I'm going to go speak with the bartender in a few minutes. He can confirm if this is the guy Lily was with."

"Good idea," Wren said. She swiped her card, and they moved into the hotel room. Ava wouldn't be able to check into her own room for hours, but at least at the moment, they could leave her suitcase and belongings here.

"He's coming inside?" Ava asked, slanting her a look as Luke walked right in and set the suitcase down.

"Luke was here earlier. We didn't sleep together," Wren quickly added. Her cheeks pinkened, and she didn't miss the amusement on Luke's face. Ava was still looking slightly bewildered.

"I stopped by this morning with coffee," Luke explained. "Wren and I spent several hours together last night discussing the case. We went over some more things earlier."

Wren didn't miss the way Ava relaxed slightly. "So all of you are former military?"

"Yes. We work for a security company now and are here in Cancun looking for Wren's sister. Wren and I bumped into each other once or twice last night before we realized we were both looking for Lily."

"This is insane," Ava said, pacing the small hotel room. "All of it. Your sister was kidnapped; her friends are missing, too. I fly down to Mexico to help my best friend and run into the jerk I spent a night with in Paris." She shook her head.

"Sam's a good guy," Luke interjected.

"He's a dick. I'm here to help Wren find her sister, but I don't want anything to do with Sam. Ever."

"Understood," Luke said, exchanging a glance with Wren. "The guys and I work together on the same team," Luke continued, "but you won't need to deal with him. It's best if you both stay here at the resort anyway."

"Not happening," Wren said.

"There's plenty that can be done here where it's safe," Luke stressed.

"Where's this picture you have to show us?" Ava asked. "Wren rushed down to Cancun so quickly, I barely know what's going on."

"Lily was communicating with a man online when she was back home, and they were here together a few days ago." Wren quickly brought Ava up to speed, explaining the rest. She pulled up a screenshot of the photo from the bar with Lily's hand at the edge of the picture.

"What a disgusting asshole!" Ava exclaimed. "He posted this online? He can't just kidnap teenage girls and get away with it. Where is he?"

"That's exactly what we're trying to find out. Let me show you what our IT guys sent." Luke showed them both the profile shot of YankeesE. Wren bristled slightly, staring at the relatively normal looking man. He was around fifty, with some gray in his dark hair. He was fit but otherwise looked like an average guy, standing there at the bar. You'd never know the evil lurking within. "His nose is crooked," she commented.

"We noticed that, too. It's a good identifying feature. I'd guess from looking at this that he's around six-feet tall. He's a Marine and in good shape. If you see him anywhere at the resort, don't confront him," Luke ordered. "I'd tell you not to look for him at all and let us handle it, but I doubt you'd sit here in your hotel room."

"Not a chance," Wren agreed.

Luke sighed. "We don't know what he's capable of, so you need to be extremely careful. He orchestrated the meeting with Lily and whisked her out of the country without anyone's knowledge. He sold her. My teammates and I are going to visit additional nightclubs this evening that are affiliated with the trafficking ring. If your sister is there, we'll exfiltrate her. In the meantime, we'll spread out around the resort today. He's still here," Luke said, looking fiercely at Wren.

"Well let's go!" she said, readying to leave. "We're

wasting time."

Luke quickly grabbed her arm, and the heat from his touch coursed through her. He looked surprised for a beat as well and cleared his throat. His thick fingers lightly caressed her forearm, soothing her, before his hand fell away. "My team is looking for him. I need you to promise me you won't confront him though. It's not safe."

Wren closed her eyes, letting out a frustrated sigh. This time Ava lightly touched her arm. "We'll go look for him, too. We'll be careful. That's why I flew down to Cancun, right? If he's still at this resort, he can't hide from all of us." Her gaze landed on Luke. "So when you find him, you think he'll just tell you what happened to Lily?"

Luke's fists clenched. "He will. He'll be arrested when we're back in the States. The guys and I work off the books, however. We'll handle it and find the missing girls."

"Let's go look around the resort," Wren urged. "I hate standing here doing nothing." Anxiety coursed through her. It felt like they were so close yet still so far. Clues were falling into place. They had a picture to work from. They just needed to find him. She couldn't stomach knowing her sister might be in pain. Hurt. Hungry. Terrified. If they had a possible lead, they needed to jump on it. She wanted to spare her sister another second of whatever awful things she was enduring.

"Okay. I just need to quick visit the restroom," Ava said, tilting her head toward it and then moving across the hotel room. She grabbed her purse and disappeared a moment, the bathroom door clicking shut behind her.

Luke stayed where he was, eyeing Wren. She swallowed, brushing some of her hair back. "We're going to find him," he said, seeming to realize how distressed she was. "While it sucks that he's enjoying a vacation while your sister is God knows where, I'm glad he keeps posting those stupid pictures. We know he's still in Mexico."

"Right. You're right," she said, tears smarting her eyes. "It's just—what if Lily is hurt? Those men wouldn't have taken her for innocent reasons. They kidnapped her for their own sick purposes." The tears spilled over, and suddenly Luke was moving closer, collecting her in his muscular arms. She relaxed against him for a moment, soaking in his strength and warmth. His woodsy scent filled her nostrils, and it was calming. Safe. One large hand palmed the back of her head; the other wrapped around her waist, anchoring her to him. Inexplicably, his lips brushed against the top of her head.

"We'll find her," he murmured, holding her close. "Don't cry. We don't know anything for certain until we have eyes on your sister. If she needs medical attention or other help, we'll get it. She'll have you and your parents encouraging her when we get her back home. She's young and resilient. We're closing in, and I don't doubt that we'll locate her."

Wren pulled back slightly, looking up into Luke's piercing blue eyes. He kept one arm securely around her waist, but he lifted his other hand and thumbed away her tears. He was so gentle with her, she almost wanted to cry harder. Luke's touch was so sweet, and her sister was no doubt enduring hell, a prisoner of cruel men. Wren didn't even understand what was happening between her and Luke at the moment, but the way he looked at her made her heart flutter.

"You seem certain that we'll find her," Wren finally said.

Luke didn't let go of her, just explained what he knew. "With the way this particular ring operates, I strongly believe she and the other teenagers are at one of the nightclubs. Hey," he said, wiping away another tear. "We'll spread out tonight to investigate the others on our list. If we find YankeesE before then—"

"You'll arrest him?" she asked. "Hurt him?"

Luke didn't answer right away, just searched her gaze. "You don't need to be afraid of me."

"I'm not," she insisted. "But how will you make this guy tell you where she is?"

"Just let me handle that part," he said evasively. "The government trusts us to get the job done. We were tasked by them to bring the girls home, and I swear to you it'll happen. We're still at the stage of gathering intelligence, but we'll find them."

The bathroom door opened, and Luke released her, stepping away. "Oh, sweetie," Ava said, rushing over as she saw that Wren was in tears. "We'll find that asshole who kidnapped her. Hell, I'll rip his balls off myself if I have to. That guy doesn't know who he's dealing with."

Luke's lips quirked slightly as he glanced between the two women. "Let's head down to the lobby together. We'll split up, but call me if you notice anything," he said, his gaze intense as he looked at Wren. "My team and I will be searching the resort as well. I'll touch base with you later, and we can compare notes. Sound all right?"

She nodded, and then the three of them were

headed back toward the elevator. Wren's heart thudded in her chest, and she drifted closer to Luke without thought. His large hand landed at the small of her back, and she couldn't help the small sigh that escaped. They needed answers, but at least for the moment she didn't feel so alone.

Chapter 13

Luke muttered a curse the next evening as he finished dinner with his teammates. Despite searching two clubs last night and keeping eyes on the resort, YankeesE and the missing teenagers hadn't materialized. They were hitting the remaining nightclubs on their list from the Feds tonight, and Luke had a feeling he wouldn't be able to convince Wren to stay back at the hotel again. He didn't like the idea of her potentially being in danger, but there wasn't much he could do to stop her. If he went alone, no doubt she'd simply follow them again.

He and his teammates had pored over data on the trafficking ring today, coming up with a list of other possibilities in the event tonight didn't pan out. There'd been no sightings of Lily or the other teenage girls, and he was itching to have a location. It was damn hard to formulate a plan and stage a rescue when you didn't know where the package was being held.

"You look pissed off," Nick commented.

"I am. We've been in country forty-eight hours and still don't have them. We need a location on the teenagers. Those girls are most likely going through hell."

"We've scouted out the initial four clubs. You know the plan was to gather intelligence first before we moved in. The Feds didn't have a handle on this, only a list of possibilities," Nick said. "Usually, we have all the data we need before an op."

Luke scrubbed a hand over his face. "Shit. Yeah. I just wish we'd split up days ago to cover more ground. This is taking too damn long."

"And potentially missed them by only having one man at each location? You know how crowded those places are. We needed multiple eyes on each nightclub to conduct a thorough search."

"Some of the girls we saw last night are younger than Lily," Sam said quietly. "It killed me to leave them there. We'll tip off the Mexican government after the op is complete, but I doubt they give a shit. The police won't do anything since the cartels and trafficking rings essentially have them on their payroll."

Luke shook his head, his stomach churning. It was impossible to rescue everyone, but that didn't make their job easier. No one deserved to live a life like that.

"Jett said Juan Lopez's name came up earlier when West was pulling open-source information on the region," Ford said.

"No shit?" Nick asked. "What for?"

"Two members of a local drug cartel were found

dead in an alley early this morning. Although Juan's group traffics people, the groups each have their own turf. Apparently, they crossed into his ground. It's believed his men offed the other two."

Luke's jaw ticked. He'd tried to warn Wren of how dangerous these men were. They'd take her in an instant as well, even if she was older than the teenagers they preferred. If she was caught snooping around somewhere she didn't belong, she could be raped or killed. Just the idea of a man hurting her made him see red. "I don't think I'll be able to convince Wren to stay here tonight," he admitted.

"You sure as shit won't convince Ava to do a damn thing," Sam said. "That woman has a mind of her own and isn't afraid to tell anyone in a ten-block radius what she's thinking."

Nick chuckled. "What's with you two? You've been sulking since she showed up yesterday. Was she such a good fuck that you can't get her out of your mind?"

"Enough," Sam ground out, glaring at his friend. "Don't talk about her that way."

Nick smirked, leaning back in his seat. "Sure thing, man. Maybe get your head out of your ass and go apologize to her then. If looks could kill, you'd be a dead man."

"Easier said than done," Sam muttered.

"Jesus," Luke said. "We don't have time for this shit now. Whatever happened between you two is in the past. We've got three teenagers we need to find. It's already all over the news. We're running out of time. If this doesn't play out like we expect tonight, we'll have to expand the search. Get a list of clients that paid for girls at the auctions and go search their homes or hotel rooms. Conduct surveillance on the homes of the trafficking ring members. The missing teenagers are here somewhere in Cancun, and we're not flying home without them."

Gray took a pull of his beer, quietly watching Luke. "So we'll split up again tonight," he confirmed. "Cover both remaining clubs on the list from the Feds. We might have to consider putting a man on the inside."

Luke's gaze slid to his. "I hate the idea of fucking around like that, but you're right. If this doesn't pan out, we can pretend we have merchandise to move." His stomach churned. Even playing the part of a man like YankeesE was disgusting. And who were the girls Luke would be pretending to sell? It's not like there were any waiting in the wings for the job. He shook his head, frowning.

The female bartender that Sam had been flirting with the other night walked by their table, waggling her fingers at Sam as she recognized him. "You never called me," she said, pretending to pout. "I thought you might be interested in hooking up."

"Sorry, sweetheart. We've been out at the clubs the past few nights," Sam said, flashing her a smile. "Don't worry. I've still got your number."

"What did you think of the place I told you about? I heard they have some new girls there," she added with a wink.

The men watched her walk away before Luke's head swiveled back toward his buddies. "Did you hear that? New girls?"

Gray was frowning, watching as the woman sashayed off to tend bar. "She could be baiting us. Maybe she knows the goons that work there and wants to send us back."

"I don't know," Luke said. "We were there the other night and nothing happened. If anything, they seemed eager for our money. Those assholes weren't exactly ushering us out."

"Ain't that the truth," Nick muttered. "All those clubs count on tourist dollars. Booze. Drugs. Women. The cartels and trafficking rings in the area know they can make serious money off Americans vacationing here."

Luke's phone buzzed on the table, and he picked it up, frowning.

Wren: *Check YankeesE's feed on the app.*

Wren: *That's Lily.*

Luke opened the app, rage coursing through him as he stared at the photo. A man's hand was gripping a woman's wrist, and the tattoo of a lily was clearly evident. They were in a crowded bar or nightclub, the lights and people evident in the background. His heart pounded, and he could hear the thumping in his ears as anger pulsed through him. "Mother fucker," he spat out.

"What's wrong?" Sam asked.

Luke turned the phone around, holding it up to show his friends, his blood boiling. "Wren just texted me. This was posted a few minutes ago."

"That's her?" Sam asked angrily, leaning closer.

"It's Lily. This must've been from last night. Why the fuck is he posting a photo like this?"

"He knows we're looking for him," Gray said, narrowing his gaze. "He has her and knows that someone is in Cancun searching for Lily and the missing teenagers. He's taunting us. Showing us that she's his."

"She's not his," Luke ground out. He was so tense, he felt like he was going to snap at any instant. She was just a teenager. Practically a child. And to have a grown man, a goddamn U.S. Marine officer, pulling her around like a piece meat was disgusting.

"It looks like they're at the club from the first night," Ford said. "Look at the lights on the stage in the background. They're similar in shape and spacing, including the one that was broken."

"We were there and didn't find her," Luke said, clenching his fist.

"We weren't at that club last night," Gray pointed out. "We were checking out two others on the list. Maybe she was still being held here at that point. Once he got word people were looking for Lily at the resort, he sold her. It'd be too risky to keep her here at the hotel. Too easy for us to get her if he thought we were moving in."

"She could've been held in his hotel room for days," Luke said, his stomach turning at the implications of that. "He kept her to himself and then sold her to the trafficking ring. Shit. Shit. Shit. We've been searching the nightclubs and should've been tearing this goddamn place apart. We've got to get over to the club," Luke said.

Gray pinned him with a look. "She could be there, or he could just want us to show up so he can see who's looking for him."

"Well then we fucking will," Luke spat out. "Except I'll head there alone so we don't draw attention to ourselves. You can follow later on."

"You're not going there alone," an angry female voice said from beside him.

Luke's head swiveled, and he saw Wren and Ava

124

standing there, fire in Wren's dark eyes. She was dressed for a nightclub unlike the other evening, wearing skinny jeans and a tight top. The outfit showed off her curves and ass to perfection, and he tried to ignore the way his blood suddenly heated. "It's not safe—"

"I don't give a shit," Wren said, interrupting him. "I was there the other night. I saw the goddamn picture. I'll find her myself if I have to. Lily's not spending another second with that monster."

Chapter 14

Wren couldn't interpret the look on Luke's face as he huffed out a frustrated sigh. He looked better than he should in a casual navy shirt that showed off his muscular frame and broad shoulders, but it was the sudden warning in his eyes that made her pause. "It's not safe," he repeated. "We went over this earlier. I know she's your sister and you want to do everything you can to save her, but it's best to let us handle this."

"He's right," Gray said, scowling. "Going there yourself is a bad idea. Luke can't keep you safe and worry about rescuing Lily."

"I'll be fine," she said stiffly.

Luke was already standing up from the table, pulling out his wallet and tossing down some cash. The rest of the men were doing the same, and she didn't miss the way Sam looked over at her friend. Ava purposefully ignored him, her gaze scanning the restaurant, her foot impatiently tapping on the floor.

Luke turned to Wren, still much taller than her despite the fact she had on heels tonight. His eyes heated for a moment as his gaze flicked over her, but it was gone so quickly, she almost wondered if she'd imagined it. "We don't know if Lily's still there. I'm guessing the photo is from last night. You know as well as I do that we were searching other locations then. He could be baiting us."

"It looks exactly like the nightclub I went to the day I arrived in Mexico. The one you guys were at where we bumped into each other."

"It does," he said with a nod.

"Then let's go," she said, grabbing Luke's arm before he could rush off without her. The heat from his skin burned into her fingertips, and she could feel his muscles tensing beneath her hand. His scent filled the air between them, and she tried to ignore the sudden electricity coursing through the air. "I came down here to find her."

Luke looked down at Wren's hand on his forearm and then back up at her. "This could be a trap. He might realize that someone is looking for him."

"I don't care. I didn't come all this way to leave her in some nightclub in Cancun while I sit around relaxing in a luxury resort. Not that I could actually relax. She's my little sister. I'm going with or without you."

He clenched his jaw but nodded, seeming to realize she wasn't backing down. Wren let go of his arm, immediately missing Luke's strength and warmth. She couldn't just stand here clinging to him though. "Ava, are you coming?" she asked.

"We'll both come," Sam said. "It'll look less

suspicious than two big guys showing up on our own, especially if this guy got tipped off that we've been asking around the resort about Lily. The four of us can go together."

"No way," Ava said, glaring at the other man. "I'm not going anywhere with you."

Sam raised his eyebrows. "Not even if it helps us find Lily?"

Ava muttered something under her breath. "Fine. But I'm sitting beside Wren in the cab. You can ride up front or something. Maybe even walk there."

"Ha ha," he muttered. "If we go there together, you're stuck with me, honey."

"I can handle myself."

"I think I handled you just fine in Paris," Sam said, licking his lips as his gaze raked over her.

"Don't be a dick," she told him. "That was a year ago, and you made your lack of interest in anything else perfectly clear. Besides, a gentleman would never kiss and tell."

"Well. who says I'm a gentleman?" he asked with a smirk.

"Enough," Wren said, growing frustrated. "Maybe both of you should just stay here if all you're going to do is argue."

"We'll be good," Ava said, giving Wren a quick hug.

Luke quietly spoke with his teammates as Wren shot her friend a look to behave, and then the foursome was moving across the lobby. "What were you guys talking about?" Wren asked.

"Just making a plan and a backup plan. We'll scout out the place and see how many men are working there tonight. If we have to create a distraction, we'll do it. The others can move in and search the back rooms. They usually keep the girls at the same clubs, according to our FBI source."

"And if that doesn't work?" she asked worriedly.

"Then we wait for the auction. Shit. The bartender even told us the club had new girls. Yo, Sam!"

"What's up?" his friend asked.

"What's the bartender's connection to all this? You got her name and number, right? Send it to West so we can run a background check on her."

"Good call," he said, pulling out his cell phone.

Ava was rolling her eyes as Luke got in the cab line. "Of course, he got the bartender's number," she muttered. "He's a total womanizer."

"Just chill out for tonight," Wren said. "We're so close to finding her."

"I got your back," Ava promised.

Wren eyed her friend but didn't respond. Ava was a talented artist but not a former Special Forces operative like Luke and Sam. There was only so much that she could do. Having more people watching the crowd in the nightclub would be helpful, but when push came to shove, the guys would be the ones saving her sister.

A cab pulled up to the curb, and then Luke was guiding the women forward as Sam climbed into the passenger seat up front. He gave the driver the name of the club, the man responding. "Si. Si. No good English."

"Do you think Lily was there all this time?" Wren asked as they climbed into the cab. She was sandwiched between Luke and Ava, and she shivered slightly at the feel of Luke's large body against hers.

"No. I think she was in his room at the resort. He

moved her last night."

"In his room?" Her stomach roiled as the implication of that washed over her. Wren gulped, and she clasped her hands together. "What about her friends?" she asked quietly.

Sam turned around from the front seat. "They weren't at the resort. So far, we have zero leads or indication that they were even in Mexico."

"Well, where are they then?" Wren asked, biting her lip.

"That's what we're trying to find out," he muttered.

Luke's phone buzzed, and Wren frowned as he spoke with whoever was on the other line. "You found additional footage? Yeah. Run it through whatever systems you have available. Let's ID this guy."

"West found more footage of him," Luke said unnecessarily. He swiped the screen of his phone after he ended the call, frowning. Tilting it toward her, Luke showed her another screenshot of YankeesE. It was slightly blurry, presumably because he'd been walking down the hall. "Our guys will enhance this," he explained. "We can run it through the databases since the profile shot hasn't given us any matches."

Wren swallowed, and Luke's gaze slid to hers. "You okay?"

"Fine. Just freaking out a little," she said, rubbing her palms on her jeans.

"Check your messages," he told Sam. "We've got another image."

The taxi continued driving through the streets of Cancun, and Luke took Wren's hand, his large one wrapping around her own. She let out a shaky breath as their hands rested on her denim-clad thighs. He might be a hardened warrior, but he was attuned to her in a way she didn't entirely understand. He'd calmed her the other night, too, resting his hand over hers on the cab ride back. Luke had held her in his arms. Briefly, she wondered if he was like this with other women he met on missions. She doubted it. Luke wasn't a player and wasn't hitting on her, trying to get her into his bed. He genuinely seemed concerned.

His thumb slid over her skin, sending shivers racing down her spine. Why did his touch feel so good? Luke was essentially a stranger. A man she'd met mere days ago. She clung to him anyway, her anchor in the midst of the turmoil.

Ava glanced over at them, noticing their joined hands, but didn't comment. At least she wasn't bickering with Sam any longer.

Fifteen minutes later, they were walking through the club's front doors. Luke's hand rested on the small of Wren's back, his fingers grazing her bare skin as her shirt shifted. Her breath caught, and then he was sliding his hand to her hip possessively. "Don't look, but we're being watched," he said in a low voice, his mouth hovering near her ear. Sam had clearly noticed the same thing, his arm wrapping around Ava's shoulders. She stiffened but then settled as he spoke quietly to her.

"There are two guys to the right of the largest bar. They recognize us," Luke said.

"Well, shit," she whispered.

Luke chuckled despite himself. "We knew that would be an issue. We weren't exactly in here unnoticed the other night. Just don't look in their direction. We're here to have a good time like everyone else. Sam was right. With you and Ava here, it just looks like we brought dates. Don't go trying to sneak into the back hallway though."

"Right, since that worked out so well before," she hissed.

Luke smirked as he squeezed her hip. "Be good," he muttered, his lips at her ear again. Wren resisted the urge to shiver. Something about Luke's closeness sent licks of heat coursing through her. She was anxious about what they mind find tonight—her sister, the men who'd taken her, the evil lurking within this place. She couldn't deny Luke's hands on her felt good though.

They crossed to the crowded bar, ordering drinks. She didn't miss the way Luke looked around and stood protectively behind her. He was alert and aware of his surroundings, a warrior ready for anything. Wren's gaze scanned the dance floor, and she heard Sam telling Ava about the auction later on. Her friend looked horrified but clearly understood the gravity of the situation. Luke gestured to Sam, but Wren didn't catch what was happening. Both men had clearly noticed something, and she stiffened.

"You're safe," Luke murmured. She relaxed into him, not minding in the least the way his muscled arm snaked around her waist. They were supposed to be a couple, just enjoying themselves for the night. Her attraction to Luke was real though, and the careful way he watched her made Wren think he felt it, too.

"I can't believe you came here by yourself the other night," Ava said. "This place is sleazy as hell."

"I can't believe Lily is here," Wren retorted.

"Shit. I know. We'll find her though. The other guys are coming, right?"

Sam nodded, and Ava seemed to relax a fraction.

Luke handed Wren a beer, and she lifted it to her lips, taking a long pull. She wasn't much of a beer drinker, but clearly, he'd had the same thought she did the other night. It was safer to purchase a bottled beverage than a drink anyone could slip something into. He was already pulling some money from his wallet and tossing it onto the bar to cover all four drinks. Luke moved to confer with Sam for a moment, and Ava sidled up next to Wren.

"You two look awfully cozy tonight," Ava teased.

Wren took a pull of her beer, smiling. "He's nice."

Ava snorted. "Uh-huh. Nice. That's why he hasn't been able to keep his hands off of you the entire time I've been here in Cancun. Something's going on," she whispered. "Don't try to deny it."

"Nothing's going on. After we find Lily, that will be that. We'll go back to New York and live our lives."

"Wait—Luke and Sam are in New York, too?"

"An hour north of the city," Wren confirmed.

"Well damn. I hate even mentioning this given the reason we're here, but you two look good together. Luke's protective of you."

Wren rolled her eyes. "I barely know him. We had dinner together one night to compare notes and coffee once when we talked with his boss. We were discussing my missing sister the entire time. For all I know, Luke acts this way with all the women he meets."

"No way. I don't believe that for a second."

Wren shrugged. "He hasn't once mentioned seeing

each other when we're back in the States or keeping in touch. He's single, from what I gather, but he's given no indication he wants to date."

"Men are dumb," Ava said. "Look how Sam promised to call and then ghosted me. Luke probably just hasn't figured out what he wants. If they're seriously only an hour away from the city, I bet you'll see him again. You guys already exchanged numbers, right?"

"Well yeah, but we've been texting about my sister."

"And he brought you coffee. Checked in to make sure you were okay. He might not admit it, but he's interested, hun. Actions speak louder than words."

"We'll see."

"Yes we will," Ava said with a wink.

The men moved back toward them, looking tense. "It looks like they're watching the back hallway tonight," Sam said, cocking his head that way without turning around. Wren hastened a gaze toward the hall she'd snuck down and noticed two men standing there. She kept her eyes moving, not wanting them to know she was looking. It was definitely some of the men from the other night.

Suddenly, Luke lifted his hand to his earpiece, his piercing gaze on Wren as he listened to the update. "Roger that. Head here first. Over."

"What's going on?" she asked.

"There's a new photo. We believe she's definitely in the nightclub."

"Seriously?" Wren fumbled with her purse, grabbing her phone and pulling up the social media app. "You're right. He posted another photo," she said, feeling distraught as she and Luke both stared at the image. Wren had no idea if the skimpy lingerie in the picture belonged to her sister or not. It didn't matter. Part of a rope was visible in the photo, as well as a cell phone. Lily's phone. Although it could've been photoshopped, the date and time were on the home screen. It had been taken minutes ago. Wren began to tremble as her gaze darted to the back of the club. "Why would he post this? And how do we know the picture is from one of the rooms here?"

"Sam got a glimpse into several rooms the other night," Luke said gently. "They're all decorated the same for the girls to service their…clients."

"Oh my God," she said, suddenly feeling weak.

"I couldn't get in because they noticed you sneaking down the back hall. I was hoping to plant a bug in there to find out more," Sam said. "We saw the women they were auctioning off, but I'd love to know the ins and outs of this operation. I doubt the same girls are brought out every night."

"So you think Lily is back there right now?" Ava said. "Let's go! Why are we just standing around?"

"Not so fast," Sam said, raising a hand to stop her. "We need to wait for our teammates to arrive. We'll remain here to keep watch and neutralize any threats while they breach and access the back rooms. We may need to subdue some of the men out here or at the very least create a distraction. All of us going back there at once could be deadly."

Ava paled slightly. "Neutralize any threats?"

"Yeah, sweetheart. You may not like me at the moment, but we're good at what we do. We're not going to risk this operation by rushing back there. You ladies really shouldn't be here at all, but that's neither here nor there at the moment." He shook his head. "Jett's girl was impulsive, too."

Wren looked at him in disbelief. "Your boss?"

"Yep. She got herself into trouble, but I guess it worked out okay. They're engaged, and she works for Shadow Security now."

"Well damn," Ava muttered.

Luke lifted his hand to speak into his mic, notifying his teammates about the number of club bouncers and employees they'd observed so far. Wren was shocked at how calm he seemed, how this was just another night to them. Maybe it was. They jetted off on dangerous missions around the world all the time. She was out of her element. Sure, she loved a good story, but she generally hadn't been in danger.

Several Mexican men walked by, their heads swiveling left and right as they checked out the crowd. One of them slowed down, studying a clubgoer around the same height and weight as Luke. "Let's dance," Luke said, suddenly pulling Wren into his arms. She gasped in surprise, and he lowered his head to her ear. "They're still watching us. Play the part." She trembled at the feel of Luke's big hands on her but didn't resist as he pulled her closer. The music had abruptly switched to a slower song, and he held her against him, the heat from his body soaking into her.

Wren snaked her arms around Luke's neck, her breasts pillowing against his broad chest. "Where are Sam and Ava?" she asked, her voice slightly breathless. Luke was hard everywhere she was soft, and they fit together in a way that made it feel like he was made just for her. They were just playing a game though. Pretending to be a couple. He'd said so himself. Once they rescued Lily, the illusion would vanish.

"They're still at the bar," Luke said, nodding in that direction. "It's best if we split up to distract the bouncers and other men who work here. Don't worry. She's safe with him."

"Yeah, but is Sam safe from her? Never mind. What time are your other friends getting here?"

"They're already on their way." He gestured to Sam, who'd clearly heard the same update as Luke. The large man was already eyeing the back of the club. "ETA is ten minutes. We're going to need to draw as many of these men out as we can. I don't like that you and Ava are here. It's dangerous."

"Well, you said yourself that it makes you look less conspicuous to have a date with you. I'd do anything for my little sister. And Ava? She's my best friend."

"What happened with her and Sam anyway?" Luke asked, quirking a brow. His gaze flicked briefly around the club again, observing, but then his intense gaze landed back on her. His large hand splayed her lower back, and even wearing heels, she still had to look up at him. Luke looked rough, and raw, and real. Her breath caught. He licked his lip, and she had a feeling that if they weren't in the middle of a mission, he'd kiss her. She felt herself flushing, trying to focus on the conversation at hand.

"I guess men don't share their feelings like women do, huh? He ghosted her. They exchanged numbers after they'd spent twenty-four hours together. They spent the night together in Paris at her hotel. Ava texted him a few times afterwards since they'd planned to keep in touch and get together when they were both back in the States. He never replied, not even to say he wasn't interested. She sent him one last text, and that was that. She never heard from him once."

Luke was frowning by the end of her explanation.

Wren looked around when he didn't reply. Ava and Sam seemed to be getting along well enough at the moment, but her friend still looked annoyed. "That picture," she said, looking up at Luke once again. "Why would he post that?"

"He wants to see who comes. Who's looking for him."

A dark-haired man with tattoos was circling the dance floor, looking at everyone. Wren resisted the urge to shiver as Luke held her close. The guy skeeved her out, and she wondered if he was one of the men who worked here. Luke seemed to have no trouble marking them. She began to feel uneasy. Suddenly, the hair on the back of her neck stood up as she spotted an American man sipping a whiskey at the bar. He was in his early fifties and had a hardened look on his face, with shortly cropped hair and a five o'clock shadow. As he set his drink back down, Wren gasped.

"What's wrong?" Luke asked, instantly alert.

"It's him," she said, trembling slightly. Luke turned them as they danced, looking over Wren's shoulder, his gaze hard. She hastened a glance back. A woman in a skimpy dress was being led to YankeesE by one of the Mexican men, and the American licked his lips as his eyes tracked over her. He held out a hand, pulling her closer.

"Fuck. His face matches the profile shot from the surveillance footage. He might even be wearing the same shirt from the most recent images. That's our guy." Luke shifted, speaking into his mic. "Nine

138

o'clock, Sam. Our mark is here. He's seated at the bar. Stand by."

"Roger that."

Anger surged through Wren, her entire body stiffening in rage. Before Luke realized what was happening to stop her, she pulled away, rushing toward the asshole who'd kidnapped her sister. She teetered on her heels, dodging people on the dancefloor and wishing she'd been wearing boots to kick this asshole right in the nuts. The woman beside him looked absolutely terrified, not to mention barely older than Lily. Wren only gave her an assessing glance before her fiery gaze landed back on him. YankeesE hadn't shaved, but she didn't miss the few scratch marks on his cheek or the leering gaze he gave the young woman. He looked up at Wren in surprise as she shouted at him, and without thought, she slapped him across the face, her hand stinging from the impact.

Chapter 15

"What the fuck?" Luke muttered, cursing as he moved around dancing couples and rushed after Wren. Most people were ignoring what was happening but a few looked over as Wren's voice rose. Luke bodily moved one guy out of the way, who started cursing at him, but Luke's vision tunneled, shock exploding within him as Wren smacked YankeesE across the face.

"Well that sure as shit was a distraction," Sam said coolly over their comms units. "The whole place will be watching us momentarily."

Wren was waving her hands in the air, yelling as Luke got closer. "Where is she? God damn it! Tell me what you did to her!"

"Look, I don't know you, lady," the guy was saying as he stood up from his barstool, trying to maneuver Wren away from him. "I don't know what you're talking about." Several of the club's bouncers were moving toward them, and Luke surged forward.

"Enough," he murmured, his large hand covering Wren's mouth as he pulled her back against him. Her slender frame crashed into his, and he couldn't ignore the way her perfect ass now pressed against his dick. Not that he had time to appreciate the feel of her in his arms right now. "Sorry, man. My girlfriend thought you were someone else."

"What is she, blind?"

"Nah, she's had a few drinks," he said, holding onto her as every muscle in his body tensed. He heard Sam speaking into his earpiece as the bouncers moved closer, updating the rest of the team. Luke was so keyed up, he could barely make out the words. Normally he felt in control on ops, able to put everything else out of his mind. With Wren here, potentially in danger, he was seeing red.

"You two, out of here!" one of the bouncers yelled. Wren was shaking, Luke's hand still covering her perfect lips. He was surprised she didn't try to bite him as keyed up as she'd been, but Wren had frozen in place as the men moved toward them.

"Let's go, baby," he said, removing his hand but gripping her hip tightly in warning. "I'll get you back to our hotel. We don't need to hang out here tonight." And then Luke was walking her to the door exactly like he had two days ago, moving her quickly through the crowd. The bouncers were talking rapidly in Spanish behind them, Luke only catching a few words. Clearly, they wanted him gone. He hastened a glance back, noting the way they glared at him.

"Ava and I are good," Sam said quietly into his mic. "We'll keep watch out here. After they search the rooms, I'll hand Ava off to you and get this fucker."

"We're in position in the back alley," Nick told them. "Ready to move in."

"It's quieted down here," Sam said. "Our guy sat back down but seems a little skittish now, looking around. I'm concerned that he might bolt. Luke, you'll keep watch out front?"

"Roger that," he confirmed.

"And I've got eyes on the back doors," Ford confirmed from his position. "Give them a few minutes to search the rooms, and it'll be over. We'll move in to grab YankeesE once we retrieve the package."

Luke held Wren roughly as they moved further away from the man they'd been hunting. His teammates could handle themselves, but that didn't mean he wanted to miss out on the action. They were so damn close, and Wren had nearly blown their cover.

"I'm sorry," Wren murmured, clearly sensing that Luke was upset.

"Nothing we can do about it now," he said, grinding his teeth.

They were a few steps from exiting the building when he slowed, sensing a hint of danger in the air. Ripples of tension coursed through Luke, his body warning him of trouble. Suddenly, a loud explosion ripped through the air, rocking the entire nightclub. Luke pushed Wren to the ground without thought, covering her with his body, as the building shook and debris rained down from the ceiling above them. Screams filled the air, the smell of smoke permeating the space, and the roar of a sudden fire almost deafening. Luke yanked Wren to her feet, holding onto her as she stumbled.

"Oh my God," she whimpered.

"I got you. Let's get out of here!"

People were shouting and pushing past them, the injured yelling for help. The air was already beginning to grow thick with smoke, the heat from the fire behind them intense. Glass broke as bottles and drinkware fell from the bar, and he heard dishes crash as tables were pushed over. He briefly glanced over his shoulder as he rushed her outside. Sam was already ushering Ava toward the front. Fortunately they'd been on the other side of the building and looked unharmed despite the explosion.

"Luke and I are okay. We're exiting the front of the building with Ava and Wren."

"What the hell was that?" Gray asked.

"Explosion near the bar area," Sam said. "Fuck. I don't see where YankeesE went. There's smoke and flames everywhere. Dozens of injured people. I need to get Ava out. Keep eyes on the front and back of the building. We can't let him escape."

"Roger that," Luke said calmly. "I've got eyes on the crowd out here."

"We're inside the club, readying to search the back rooms," Nick said, his voice hard to hear over the shouts and alarms that were now going off. "Lots of people are running this way, trying to exit the building. We've only got a minute or two. Damn it! The first room is locked." He yelled something to Gray.

Luke heard banging over his earpiece, and then the sound cut off. "God damn it," he muttered.

"What's happening?" Wren asked, looking around at the chaos.

"The guys were in the back when the explosion

went off. Nick and Gray have to break into the rooms to search them."

"Oh my God. What if she's trapped in there?"

"They'll find her," Luke said, his voice grim. The reality was, he had no idea what condition Lily would be in or if she was really there. There were multiple rooms to clear, and in the chaos, he didn't know how much time his friends had. They'd do what they could but didn't have oxygen tanks or equipment with them to withstand the heat and flames. They'd have to exit the building within minutes. Hell. He didn't even recall seeing a fire extinguisher inside the club, although the alarms that were now sounding were piercing. Emergency responders would be on their way soon.

Sam and Ava came rushing toward them, Sam's intense gaze sweeping the area. "Where is he?" Sam asked urgently. Ava was looking around in a panic, gripping his arm. Sirens sounded in the distance as firetrucks approached, and the sound of glass being smashed filled the air as people broke windows to get out of the building faster.

"We should go around the building to the back," Wren said. "Lily's going to be terrified." Luke glanced over, watching as she paled. Ava had now moved closer to her friend, rubbing her back comfortingly.

"It's not safe. Just let the guys search the rooms," Ava said. She brushed her strawberry-blonde hair back, looking rattled despite the calm in her voice.

"Who the hell set off the explosives?" Sam asked, looking irate.

"Seems like quite a coincidence that we spotted YankeesE moments before all hell broke loose," Luke said. "He posted a picture all but confirming her location. He expected us to move in."

"Did he make you?" Sam asked.

Luke shook his head. "I don't think so. He certainly wasn't expecting Wren to rush over and slap him. I think he's expecting the Feds. At any rate, he didn't stop the bouncers from hustling us out. If he wanted me harmed, he'd have stalled."

"Who the hell orchestrated it then? Juan Lopez's men?"

"It makes no sense that they'd blow up their own damn club," Luke pointed out.

"Unless YankeesE set off the explosives but was targeting someone else," Sam mused.

Ford came running to the front of the building, heading straight toward them. He looked lethal with a sidearm and K-BAR knife strapped to his thigh, his gaze hard. "Let's search the building to the right! I think there's another exit from the nightclub."

"What?" Luke asked sharply, glancing over to the second location.

Ford huffed out a breath, pointing. "I was in the back alley and saw some men coming from the next building. They looked like the hired guns that were here the other night. I was about to give chase, but they disappeared on me. I also lost communication with Nick and Gray."

Luke clicked on his mic. "Nick. Gray. SITREP."

There was no response, and he exchanged a glance with his teammates. Two firetrucks pulled up to the curb, sirens wailing, in addition to several ambulances. People were still streaming out of the nightclub, some crying and coughing. Multiple civilians were injured, and he heard the screams of people still trapped inside. "All right, let's head over—"

Suddenly his gaze caught on a man in a baseball cap and black leather jacket, surreptitiously looking around as he tried to slip through the crowd. He looked down toward the ground, but Luke recognized his profile. "That's him!" Luke said, his voice harsh. Sam whipped his head around and charged forward, pushing his way through the crowd and tackling YankeesE to the ground. Ford was instantly at his side, further restraining him, while Luke remained with the two women.

Nick's voice suddenly came over their earpieces.

"What was that?" Luke asked, his heart pounding in his chest. "You're cutting out. Tell me you found them."

His friend was coughing, and Luke's blood ran cold at his words. "No, man. We searched the back rooms, but they're gone. Every single room was empty."

Chapter 16

Wren's heart stuttered as Luke looked toward her. His hand was on his ear, listening to the updates from his teammates, but it was the devastation in his eyes that made her falter. "What's wrong? Is Lily okay?"

Luke shook his head. "I'm sorry. She wasn't back there."

Tears filled her eyes as Sam and Ford restrained YankeesE, pulling zip ties from their pockets to bind his hands behind his back. Ford was gesturing toward the building as he told Sam something, but Wren wasn't following what was happening. The baseball cap had fallen off YankeesE as they pinned him to the ground, and as his head turned, hard eyes met hers. She felt her breath catch, the evil emanating from his icy glare.

"But…where is she?" Wren asked Luke, feeling dazed. "He posted that picture. How could no one be back there? Where'd they go?"

"We think they took the girls out a secret exit," he explained in a low voice.

Fury filled her, temporarily replacing her sadness, and she stormed YankessE as he struggled and swore. "Easy, sweetheart," Luke said, coming after her. "Let them handle this. We're already drawing too much attention to ourselves." Big hands gripped her waist, making her breath catch. Luke pulled her back against his broad chest, but not before the other man noticed her.

"You. You're her sister, aren't you?" YankeesE snarled. "You look alike. Older, but—"

Ford silenced him, gagging the man with a piece of cloth he'd produced. For the first time, Wren noticed the people gathering around them and felt the danger in the air. Someone had pulled out a cell phone to start recording, and Wren watched in disbelief as Gray appeared out of nowhere, smashing it to the ground. "Don't look at them!" he ordered. "Mind your own damn business."

Luke kept his hands on her, and she didn't hate the way it felt to have him hold her close. Even as the world seemed to be crumbling apart, he somehow grounded her. Made her feel safe. Nick was suddenly at Gray's side, and then the men were lifting YankeesE off the ground like he weighed nothing. Ford reappeared, calling out to his teammates, "I've got a vehicle! Let's move!" Wren hadn't even realized he was gone in the confusion.

"A vehicle? I thought they took a cab like us," she said.

"Negative. They've got their own transportation. We've got to get out of here," Luke warned, moving her away. "Someone's going to notice what's going on. I don't need our photos blasted everywhere or on some hit list."

"But my sister!"

"He'll know where she is. Let my teammates handle this."

"What will they do with him?" Ava asked in surprise.

Sam leveled her with a look. "They're taking him back to our hotel for questioning. He'll be brought back to the States and arrested."

Luke's gaze was tracking the area, and he suddenly gestured to Sam. Without a word, Sam grabbed Ava's hand and tugged her across the street, disappearing around the corner. "We're splitting up," Luke explained. "They're looking for us."

Nervously glancing around, Wren noticed several of the men she'd seen days before standing about twenty feet away—muscular guys with tattoos on their arms, their hair pulled back in short ponytails. She stiffened, moving closer to Luke's big body. His warmth seeped into her, and his muscled arm wrapped around her waist once more. "Let's go. I need to get you out of here."

"What if they follow us?" she asked.

His eyes locked on hers. "I'll handle it."

Her lips parted, and suddenly he ducked down and kissed her, sending shockwaves coursing through her entire body. It was over before it had begun, but she still felt the heat of Luke's lips on hers, warmth flushing over her skin. "Why'd you kiss me?" she asked, her heart pounding wildly in her chest as she met his intense gaze.

"You looked upset."

"Luke," she pleaded.

"You're safe with me, sweetheart. Just let me get you out of here. We'll talk then." Luke lifted his hand to his ear, listening to another update, before he gently tugged Wren into a dark bar across the street. More emergency vehicles were arriving outside, the flames licking out from the side of the nightclub they'd just left. It felt like a scene from a movie, with police officers and more ambulances arriving, injured people, and of course the man Luke's teammates had taken into custody.

"Let's hang out here a bit," he said as the door swung shut behind them. People were milling about, talking as they watched the commotion outside through the windows. "Sam has Ava in a cab. I'll watch the front and then get us out when it's safe. It's best to stay out of sight at the moment."

"Safe from who? Those men?"

"Yes. They didn't see us come in here. They'll move on by. Nick bugged one of the guys in the chaos as everyone was rushing out. They're looking for YankeesE. From the sounds of it, they think he set off the explosives, destroying the nightclub."

"Why would he do that?" she asked.

"I don't know. He might've been targeting someone."

"Oh my God," she murmured, dropping her face to her hands. "This entire thing is a nightmare."

"Hey," he said softly, lightly wrapping his fingers around her wrists. He lifted her hands away so he could see her, bringing one large hand up to brush away her stray tears. "We're one step closer. We got our guy. After we question him, we'll learn her location."

"But we don't have Lily yet," she said, frustrated

tears spilling over.

"I know, honey," he murmured. Thick fingers caught another tear rolling down her cheek, and then Luke cupped her face so gently, she almost forgot to breathe. The air grew thick between them, and in that moment, Wren wanted Luke more than her next breath. She might've been upset, but he soothed something deep inside her. Grounded her. Made her feel alive in a way she never had before.

"Please don't cry," he said huskily. "I promise you that I'm not leaving Mexico without your sister."

"I know. I believe you," she whispered.

Luke didn't move away, just continued to gently thumb away her tears. She let out a soft sigh. Searching her gaze, he ducked down slowly. Maybe it was the adrenaline-fueled situation, the fear coursing through her—she wasn't sure. Wren melted against him as his lips met hers. Luke tasted of musk and man, commanding but still careful with her, his hard body pressed against her own. Maybe it was wrong to be standing here letting him kiss her when Lily was still missing, but she couldn't make herself pull away. Her body alighted under his touch, which was so damn sweet despite his gruffness. Wren needed his strength and warmth, and she clung to him like he was her lifeline.

Luke's hand pressed into the small of her back, guiding her closer. His tongue trailed over her lips, and she opened to him, letting him kiss her more deeply. The stubble on his jaw rubbed against her skin, and it felt like he was claiming her, right then and there in the crowded bar.

Wren could feel his erection against her stomach as he held her against him. Luke was big. Thick. She was clutching onto his shirt and could feel the hard muscles of his abdomen. They were both breathing heavily when he finally pulled back, Luke hastening a glance outside. The men had moved past, but they remained in place, holding onto one another. His lips hovered near her ear, his body hovering protectively over hers. "I can't seem to resist you. What are you doing to me?" he asked, one hand trailing through her hair.

"The same thing you're doing to me," she admitted.

The heat in his gaze was enough to burn her up. Luke ducked down, kissing her briefly once again. His hands slid to her hips, his thumbs rubbing in small circles, and she felt arousal dampening her panties. He was barely touching her, yet she felt all too aware of every part of him. Luke was her calm in the middle of chaos, and she reacted to him on an elemental level. He scanned the crowd outside once more, not releasing her from his embrace. "When we head back, I've got to meet with my teammates. Talk with our boss. This guy has answers that we need."

"I know. I'm scared."

"I swear to you that I'll find her. My teammates are already questioning him. Once we get out of here, I'll make sure you're safe in your room and then join them. Don't cry," he said, noticing the wetness that once again filled her eyes.

"Where'd they take him?" she asked.

"To the place we're staying at."

"I want to come, too. Please. I can wait in your room or something. This guy knows where my sister is. He hurt her. Let me stay there so I can find out what's going on."

"Wren…."

"Please."

He huffed out a sigh. "You can't be there when we interrogate him. It's not safe."

"I know," she agreed. "I understand. I just need to be where you are. He took my sister. He probably hurt her, raped her." Wren choked out the last words, and Luke pulled her closer, tucking her head against his chest.

"What about Ava? You want to leave her at the resort alone?" he pressed. She could tell he was trying to convince her not to come with him. He was right, but she hated not being there to witness them questioning the man who'd taken Lily.

"I don't know," she finally said. "I just want answers."

"I know you do. And I swear that I'll find out where Lily and her friends are."

Chapter 17

Luke crossed his arms, glaring at the man they'd captured. YankeesE had refused to talk so far, aside from briefly saying that if they harmed him, they'd never see the missing teenagers again. Luke wanted to punch the smug look right off his face. He'd be extradited back to the States soon, but they needed answers ASAP.

The man's hard eyes tracked Luke's movements around the small room. He'd seen all of their faces at the nightclub, so there was no need to keep him blindfolded during questioning or to disguise themselves. The ID he carried was fake, but Sam had already sent his photograph to Shadow Security headquarters. They'd know his true identification shortly.

"We can do this the easy way or the hard way," Luke said, nailing the asshole with a look.

The guy shifted in his seat, tensing slightly, but

remained silent.

"I don't have all night. Tell me where the teenagers from Philadelphia are. We have your communications with them. We've seen the message you send, coercing underage girls to do your biding. It' over."

YankessE leaned over and spit on the floor, still not saying a word.

Luke nodded at Nick and Sam to remain with him and then into the conference room they'd set up for a briefing with the other men. They established a secure connection on the company laptop, and a moment later, their boss's face appeared on the screen.

"You got him," Jett said unnecessarily. He looked alert despite the late hour, and Luke knew he'd be fired up on adrenaline until the girls were back in their custody. They were so close he could almost taste it. They just needed that asshole's cooperation.

"Roger that. The guys brought him back to our hotel an hour ago. He's not talking," Luke said, his fist clenching. "We still don't have a location for Lily or the other missing teenagers."

"West is here," Jett said, nodding off camera for the other man to come over. "He's got an update to share that will move things along."

West's face appeared on the screen, and he briefly said hello to Luke and his teammates. "I matched a name to the face," he told them. "It was tricky only having the profile shot before from the bar surveillance footage, but now that you sent a clear picture, our system made a match."

"You've got a name?" Luke barked. "What is it?"

"Ethan Mongrove. He's a Marine officer stationed in Quantico, Virginia, set to retire next year. He received a disciplinary action in the past but has been coasting along the past year, no doubt readying for retirement."

Luke stilled, memories of their last op several weeks ago filling his mind. The scrap of paper he'd found had a name on it—Ethan. "The op in Mexico City—where we rescued the teenage daughter of a Government official. The paper I found on the ground had the name Ethan on it along with a partial phone number."

"God damn, yes it did," Jett said, his eyes sparking with interest "Fingerprint him. There was a partial print on the paper as well. The Feds couldn't match it to anything, but this might tie the two cases together. It'll be just another nail in his coffin."

"Jesus. That wasn't Juan Lopez's group either," Luke said, wiping his forehead. "How many guys is he working with?"

"We ran a background check on him," Jett said. "We pulled the locations of where he was stationed while serving. He was TDY to Mexico several years ago. He made a significant number of foreign contacts in several Mexican cities, some reported during his security clearance reinvestigation and some not. DOD was very interested in the contacts he's made and maintained. They're running traces on his finances now to see where the money he received is going. He's been selling girls, but there's no telling if he's also been providing classified information for cash. His interest in teenage girls was lucrative for him but also self-serving. He'd addicted to pornography, given his Web history."

"Jesus. Maybe he'll be willing to talk when he realizes it's over. We know everything. He won't be enjoying retirement because he'll be in jail."

"It's over for him," Jett agreed. "I've arranged a flight for Ford and Gray to bring him back to the States. The Feds will meet them at the airport. Luke, Nick, and Sam will remain in Cancun to locate the teenagers. Get the info from him. Find the location of the girls. He's in deep with the traffickers and likely knows where they were taken."

"We'll get their location from him," Luke promised. "Although he's posted pictures of Lily, we've seen no traces of the other girls."

Jett muttered a curse. "All three of them need to be brought home. Ford filled me in earlier on the explosion at the nightclub."

"Sir," Ford said with a nod.

Jett eyed him. "The Feds are very interested in the explosion tonight. As it happens, a high-ranking military officer was visiting Cancun with his family and was believed to be in that nightclub."

"He was targeting someone?" Luke asked, surprise washing over him.

"We believe that's highly likely. A man named Michael O'Donnell was there. He's a Sergeant Major and worked with Mongrove. Ethan has made some waves over the years with the trouble he's gotten into. Although they were friends at one point, he blamed O'Donnell for some trouble he got into. This may have been retaliation for that."

"Jesus. Do we have any information on his status?"

"He reached out to the embassy. He was there supervising his two college-aged daughters and simply enjoying a family vacation from what we can tell. All three escaped unharmed."

"I'm glad they're all right," Luke said. "A large

number of people weren't as lucky. Given the number of clues that Ethan had been posting, we suspected he was trying to lure in the Feds. I thought he had a beef with the Bureau."

"Negative," Jett said, his gaze hard. "Ethan Mongrove has been disciplined before by his higher-ups. He's angry with some of his superiors for being denied a promotion. I understand O'Donnell got a job he wanted."

"So he tried to off him?" Luke asked, bewildered.

Gray rubbed his hands together, looking agitated. "Let's take this asshole to task. He thinks we still don't know anything about him? He's wrong. We'll get a location and move in. I'm ready to end this."

Luke's gaze swiveled back to the laptop screen. "Let me know when you've got an address for where the teenagers are being held," Jett ordered.

"Will do," Luke replied. "I'll inform the others that you're securing a plane for the flight." They said goodbye and ended the video call. Luke eyed his teammates. It seemed strange as hell that a fellow Marine would be down in Mexico at the same time as Ethan. Cancun might be a popular vacation spot, but still. They hadn't arrived here together. Something niggled at the back of his mind, but he couldn't quite place it.

Gray shoved his chair back and stood, drawing Luke's attention. Gray punched his fist into his open palm, his eyes darting to the wall separating them from the room Ethan was being held in.

"You okay, man?" Ford asked with a frown.

"Yeah. Just pissed as hell that the teenagers are still being held captive."

"He'll talk now," Ford said. "We've got everything

on him. We can either smooth the way for when he's taken into Federal custody, offering him some leniency in exchange for intel, or we can do this the hard way."

Luke cocked his head to the door. "Then let's roll."

***

The men watched Ethan grow angrier and angrier as they relayed the background information they'd gotten on him. With each and every detail they revealed, his face had grown harder. He still sneered every time they demanded the location of the teenage girls, thinking he had one up on them.

"It's over, asshole," Luke said, slamming his hand onto the table. "You want the Feds to know you cooperated with us? Then tell me where they are. Playing nice will behoove you in the long run. They're not in your hands now, but you can tell us where they're being kept. Who you're working with."

Ethan smirked. "I'm surprised you think they're still alive."

"Of course, they're alive. That's how those sick-as-fuck traffickers work. They need merchandise to keep their operation running. We know you've worked with Juan Lopez's group in the past. Your online accounts have already been linked to multiple other girls who've gone missing. Your offshore accounts are being tracked. Your U.S. bank accounts have been frozen. We've searched your hotel room, and the Feds are searching your home. It's over."

Ethan's gaze flicked to him, his eyes narrowing.

"When you arrive back in the States, you'll

immediately be taken into Federal custody. Soon your face will be blasted on every news channel all over the country. Your career will end in disgrace. You're a criminal and a traitor who will be dishonorably discharged from the military."

Ethan chuckled, shaking his head.

"What the fuck is so funny?" Sam asked.

"It was a hell of a way to go," Ethan said, licking his lips. "I've sunk into more ripe pussy than you'll ever dream about. Talked more teenage girls into sucking my cock than you'll ever have. You're not man enough for the things I've done."

"You're sick," Sam said.

Ethan shrugged. "I like my girls young. Teenagers aren't interested in a middle-aged man like me or Mick unless they think we can do something for them."

"Who the fuck is Mick?" Gray asked, narrowing his gaze.

Ethan lifted a shoulder. "Just another asshole who fucked me over. But don't worry, I might be willing to share his information with the Feds if they play their cards right. I've got the dirt on him. You think I'm the only sinner out there?"

"You're preying on teenagers young enough to be your daughter," Sam said, his voice harsh.

Luke crossed his arms, glaring at him. "Why'd you post all those photos now? It was easy as hell to track you here."

"It's just a game," Ethan said with smirk. "Sooner or later they'd figure it out. I've been denied what was rightfully mine—career advancement, power, promotions. Moving girls was more fulfilling—for me at any rate. They weren't always cooperative, but I got what I wanted."

Anger burst within him, and Luke pointed his finger at Ethan, every muscle in his body tense. "Where are they?"

Ethan chuckled darkly. "They're Juan's property now. All three of them. You'll never see that piece of pussy again."

"Fuck you," Sam spat out.

Luke gripped the table, his eyes blazing. "We know they're not at Juan Lopez's home. Where does he keep the girls you sell him? Maybe we should rat you out. Let Juan think you traded your freedom for information on his trafficking operation. You'll be dead before we fly out of Cancun. I'm not sure we can offer you protection unless you cooperate. It'd be a shame to leave you alone on the side of the road for whoever happens to come by."

Ethan's lips quirked. "And how will that help you find the teenagers if I'm gone? Maybe you'd consider a trade. Me for the girls."

"Hell no."

Nick rose from the seat he'd been in, moving across the room. He gestured to Gray, who followed him into the conference space they'd set up next door. Luke exchanged a glance with Sam, who lifted a shoulder.

"Wait here," Luke said, pointing at Ethan again. Not like the asshole could go anywhere while handcuffed and guarded. He turned and followed his teammates out, leaving Sam and Ford to watch the disgraced Marine.

"What do you got?" Luke asked, moving into the small room.

"We bugged one of the goons working for Juan. I

haven't heard anything for a while and thought it malfunctioned—defective equipment or whatnot. They've moved somewhere quieter now, and I can hear what's going on."

"Tell me you have a location," Luke said, adrenaline spiking through his blood.

"Affirmative. They've moved the girls from the nightclub to a building across town." Nick leaned over and typed the address into his laptop, pulling it up on a map. "There we go. We can ask West if there's any sat imagery from this area so we can assess the least busy time to move in. If Lily and her friends were in the nightclub earlier, there's a good chance this is where they all are now."

Luke's phone buzzed, and he lifted it to his ear. "I've got a flight out of an airstrip in Cancun," Jett said. "The pilot's been arranged and will be on standby. Ford and Gray will escort Ethan Mongrove back to the States. They'll be landing near JFK, where he'll be met by the Feds and taken into custody."

"Roger that," Luke said, glancing at his teammates. "We've got an update. Nick has a location where the girls may have been taken this evening after the explosion. After we get Mongrove on his way, the men and I will make preparations to move in."

"Get whatever intelligence you need and end this," Jett ordered.

"Yep. We're on it. Talk to you soon, boss." Luke ended the call, looking at his buddies. "Call West," he told Nick. "Let's get whatever intel we can on the new location. Sam, pull up what's available online via open sources and Google maps. Let's get entry and exit points and notes on the surrounding area. Street names, traffic lights, everything. Gray, let's go tell

Ford he's flying out tonight. Mongrove now has a one-way ticket back to U.S. soil, and we'll deliver him to the Feds wrapped up in a fucking bow."

Chapter 18

Two hours later, Wren rubbed her eyes, the stress from the evening weighing on her. She'd waited with Ava for a while in the hotel lobby, talking quietly about the explosion at the nightclub, both women eventually retreating to their own rooms. Wren was a gigantic ball of stress, her nerves shot. She'd texted Luke once, and he'd only given her a brief reply that they were working on things.

Working on things.

Was he still questioning YankeesE? Did they have a location for her sister? Had they found out his real name? She hated not knowing but also realized she'd only be in the way if she went to Luke's hotel. Adjusting her top, she padded across her hotel room. She'd ditched the heels the moment she'd stepped inside. Now she just felt restless. Agitated. Her parents had called earlier, and she hated that she virtually had no good news for them. Lily was still missing. That was the bottom line and all that mattered during this hellish night.

A quiet knocking on her door had her jolting in surprise, and then she hurried across the room, surprised to see Luke through the peephole. "Hey," he said in a low voice as the door swung open. "Can I come in?"

"Yeah, sure," she said, unable to resist grabbing onto his muscled forearm as she tugged him inside. His skin felt warm beneath her chilled fingertips, and she felt soothed somehow now that he was here. Calmer. If he'd shown up in person, he must have new information to share, and she could feel her heart pounding.

"You're freezing," he murmured, one large hand running down her arm. His gaze swept over her as if making sure she was okay.

"I need to turn down the air conditioning. Ava and I were hanging out in the lobby. I was too anxious to come back here and sit and wait alone," she admitted. "I just got to my room a few minutes ago. Tell me what's going on," she pleaded.

Luke blew out a sigh. "Our guys at Shadow Security ran facial recognition software on YankeesE. They got a hit now that we could provide a clear photograph. He had identification on him but was traveling with fake credentials. His real name is Ethan Mongrove. He's a Marine based in Quantico, Virginia."

"That's not too far from Philadelphia," Wren murmured. "Maybe four hours or so. He could've easily driven up there to get Lily."

"He could have, yes. Once we got a name, we passed it on to Federal officials. They'll be searching his home and confiscating his electronics to determine the number of the victims he's connected to. He's being extradited tonight. My boss got a private plane and pilot set up for us."

"You're leaving?" she asked, her heart falling.

Luke shook his head. "No. Ford and Gray are flying him back to U.S. soil to hand over. The rest of us will remain here."

"He's gone?"

Luke nodded. "He's gone. We questioned him earlier, but the Feds want him back ASAP. He's tied to several cases that we know of and will have multiple charges brought against him. Ford texted me when the plane took off. They'll turn him over upon landing."

"What about my sister?" she asked.

Luke held her gaze, the concern clear on his face. "We've got an address where we believe she's being held but are waiting on additional information before we move in. Nick and Sam are gathering data on the building schematics now as well as the surrounding area. It's late—already past one in the morning. We need a detailed layout before we conduct a rescue. The building she's being held at isn't one of the nightclubs we were investigating. We know next to nothing about it."

"How'd you find out where she is?"

"Nick was able to plant a bug on one of the bouncers earlier. We weren't close enough the other night to do so without being caught or arousing suspicion. Everyone was pushing and shoving tonight in their haste to leave after the explosion, so it afforded the perfect opportunity."

"Wow. So are you heading over there?"

"We've got a location but can't move in yet, sweetheart. They're pulling info now so we can come up with a plan and backup plan to extract your sister, but we may need to stand by until tomorrow."

"Tomorrow?" she asked, her face falling.

"I'm sorry. It doesn't make sense to fly in blind. This location wasn't on our list of targets. We don't know anything about it and need to gather data before we stage a rescue. We don't believe she's in immediate danger—not any more so than when she was held here or at the nightclub."

Wren lifted a hand to her chest, practically feeling her heart beating uncontrollably. "I understand. It just kills me to know we're so close yet leaving her there another day."

"We're one step closer," he said as tears filled her eyes.

"I know, I just—" Her voice cut off.

Luke moved closer and collected her in his arms, cradling her head against his chest. She was even shorter without her heels, and she felt him tighten his arms protectively around her. Wren felt small and feminine compared to his bulk and strength. One hand smoothed over her hair as she let out as sigh, sinking into him for comfort. "We'll do everything we can to move in quickly tomorrow. We got teams back at headquarters pulling blueprints of nearby buildings as well because it's in a busy area of the city. We want multiple exit points should they come after us. The goal is to get Lily out safely."

"I know," she said softly.

"Hey. I promise you we'll get her."

"What about Lily's friends?"

"I hope like hell they're there, too. Ethan

Mongrove wasn't willing to give us any information. As you already know, the pictures posted showed that Lily was with him. Whether he coincidentally decided to use her photos or didn't have a choice, I'm not sure. He didn't post any pictures indicating he had the other girls. Maybe they were being held elsewhere. Maybe an accomplice brought them down to Mexico. He'll be questioned by the Feds but won't be landing for hours."

She nodded, stifling a yawn. The entire night had been exhausting and overwhelming, from the explosion at the club to Luke kissing her at the bar afterwards to knowing they'd finally captured YankeesE—Ethan. He was only one piece of the puzzle though, because they still needed her sister.

"It's late. I should let you rest and head back to my hotel," Luke said quietly. "We'll be busy tomorrow, so the guys and I are all gonna grab some shut-eye as well. Our IT guys at headquarters will be working through the night. We'll brief in the morning and prepare to move in tomorrow night."

Tears filled her eyes once more. "No," she murmured, clinging to him. "I want you to stay with me."

He pulled back slightly, searching her gaze. "Are you sure? I don't want to make you feel uncomfortable."

"You make me feel safe." He pulled her close again, and she breathed in, inhaling his scent.

His fingers trailed through her hair, gently massaging her scalp. "You're smart and gutsy as hell for coming here after your sister. A lot of people wouldn't be able to do that. You tracked down where she was and flew to another country to get to her."

"I'm used to chasing down stories, but this one takes the cake. I never thought Lily would fall for something like this. She's a teenager, but I always figured she was too smart for that."

"Ethan is a predator," Luke said. "He's smart and shrewd, but he took his luck too far. Evidently, he may have been targeting another Marine officer that he learned was vacationing in Cancun. The explosion was premeditated, and we just happened to be there at the nightclub."

"He really didn't know you were looking for him?" Wren asked.

"He knew someone was. As to whether he suspected me specifically? No, I don't think he did."

"What's the name of the man he targeted?"

"Oh hell. It was Michael something or other. I'll get it from my boss and let you know. Listen, why don't you get changed or do whatever you need to do. I'll text the guys and let them know I'm staying here."

She looked up at him as she murmured okay, and Luke gently kissed her forehead. It was sweet, and despite the turmoil she felt at Lily still being gone, her heart fluttered. Luke's presence had awareness washing over her, and she glanced toward her suitcase. She had the same slinky nightgown from the other day to change into and hadn't packed other pajamas. It was silly to feel embarrassed now when she'd already invited him to stay. It's not like she'd wear the skinny jeans she had on to bed, and certainly he expected her to put on something different.

"Go ahead," Luke said, nodding toward her suitcase. "I'll quick call Sam while you get ready."

She nodded and moved to gather her things, disappearing into the bathroom. The sound of Luke's deep voice soothed her as she washed her face, and she heard him discussing a plan for the morning. They were close. So close. And tomorrow they'd have Lily.

Chapter 19

Luke blinked, momentarily forgetting where he was, before he felt Wren stirring beside him. Wren. He was in her bed, in her hotel room. He'd spent the night when she'd asked for him to stay. Nothing untoward had happened. He'd changed after she'd gotten ready for bed, stripping down to his boxers and tee shirt, and then he'd simply climbed in beside her. Felt her breathe a sigh of relief as she snuggled against him, whispering her fears about her sister. At one point during the night his phone had buzzed on the nightstand, waking them both, but it was just a brief update from headquarters. He'd scanned the message, thumbed a reply, and told Wren to go back to sleep.

Now the morning sun was coming in through the slit between the balcony door and light-blocking curtain. The rest of the room was dark, and as he glanced at the clock, he was surprised that it was already oh-seven-hundred. Luke was an early riser.

Years in the military had made it impossible to be anything else. He felt groggy in a way he hadn't in years, waking from a deep, satisfying rest. Wren shifted, her breasts inadvertently pressing further into him, and Luke felt his cock twitch. Luke closed his eyes again, enjoying the feel of her in his arms and trying to will his dick to stand down. Someday he'd love to spend an entire night exploring her curves, teasing her, and making Wren cry out his name. He had work to do today. Plans to finalize and hours to kill before they moved in.

Wren's hand moved on his chest, clinging to him even in her sleep, and a slow smile crept across his lips. "Morning," she mumbled sleepily.

He opened one eye, looking at her. "How'd you sleep?" His eyelids clamped shut again, but his hand ran over her, soothing. Luke was content. When the hell had he last felt like this? It's not like they'd had a night of mind-blowing sex. He'd simply held her. And she'd given him a sense of peace he didn't even realize he'd been missing.

"Good. Too good. Lily is still out there and we—"

"We'll get her tonight," he promised.

"I just hope she's okay," Wren whispered in the darkness. She sniffled slightly, and he held her more tightly. Luke could feel her breasts pillowed against him, her body perfectly aligned against his. She was wearing a strappy nightgown that he'd only gotten a glimpse of before he turned off the lights, but Luke swore she was the most gorgeous thing he'd ever seen. Her long, dark hair had been tousled, her smooth skin just begging to be touched. If he shifted her just so, she'd be straddling him, her heat pressed against his stiffening cock.

Except that wasn't about to happen. She was upset, and this wasn't the time for him to be having carnal thoughts. "I'm sorry," he murmured, his voice husky with sleep and desire. "I wish I could promise you that she was fine."

"You make me feel better just by holding me," Wren admitted. "I just hate that I'm safe and she's not."

"I know. I don't have any siblings but sure as hell would feel the same way as you. When Gray was taken hostage, it was brutal. My teammates and I were ready to do anything to get to him."

"What happened to him?" she asked quietly.

Luke shifted his fingers on her bare arm, tracing a pattern on her skin. "He was held in captivity. Tortured. He's not the same man he was before. He's gruffer now, less trusting. Gray was the last guy to join the team. Somehow Jett talked him into it. He's a good man though, and I'd trust him with my life."

"All of you work out of the same place?"

"Yep. It's in upstate New York, just about an hour north of the city."

"Are you there much? Or are you always flying off on missions around the world?"

"We do travel a lot," Luke admitted. "But we also have plenty of time at our home base. It's a large compound where we can train and discuss cases. Jett decides what jobs we take, but they're generally short missions. It's not like deploying when I was in the military. I want to see you when we're back in the States," he said.

"Me too."

He caught her hand in his, running his thumb over her knuckles. "We've already exchanged numbers, but

I want to take you out. On a real date," he clarified. "No comparing notes over dinner about a case."

"Just promise me no sleazy nightclubs," she said, letting her hand trail over his abs as he released her. He stiffened, his cock rising to life. He wasn't even sure Wren realized the effect she had on him. Luke was doing all he could not to frighten her by moving too quickly. His body had a mind of its own, however, and reacted on an almost primal level when she was near. Luke wanted to touch and caress her. Kiss her. Explore those tempting curves. Claim her as his.

"Not a chance," he said. "No nightclubs. I'm thinking more along the lines of a quiet dinner. I can come to the city, or you can come up to my place."

"I don't have a car," she admitted. "City life."

"Then I'll come pick you up," he immediately said. "I don't mind bringing you up to my place one weekend. We'll eat, relax, and spend some time together without being in the middle of an operation. Your sister will be home safe. Life will be good."

"You're not going to disappear on me like Sam did with Ava, are you?"

His lips brushed against the top of Wren's head, and he inhaled her floral scent. "Of course not," he said, his hand trailing over the smooth skin of her back, his fingers just slipping beneath the fabric of her nightgown. Her breath caught, and as Wren looked up to meet his eyes in the dim light, he couldn't resist taking her mouth in a soft kiss. "I plan to spend a lot of time getting to know you better when we're back in New York. All of you," he added, his voice husky. "I'm going to kiss you everywhere, learn what you like. Find out all the different ways I can make you come."

Her lips parted in surprise, her cheeks pinkening, and he kissed her again. She was so damn sweet and responsive. Luke could hardly imagine what it would be like to slowly discover all of Wren. There was a hint of shyness in her that made his protective instincts rise. He wanted to make her come apart in his arms but also just hold her. Let her know she was safe with him. "It's too soon right now—not that we have time to spend the morning in bed anyway. I'll wait until you're ready, Wren, but make no mistake—I want you."

She clung to him as he took her lips once more. Luke rolled them over, pinning her beneath him as he took control. He knew she could feel his erection, but there was no hiding it. She was sexy and beautiful beneath him in bed, her body arching up against him, demanding more. The sexy little nightgown she had on did nothing but accentuate her curves. Make him want more. He reluctantly pulled back after a minute, hovering above her. Wren was panting beneath him, her lips swollen from his kisses, but he respected her too much for a quick roll between the sheets. There'd be plenty of time to make love when they were back home. He wanted to spend his time exploring her gorgeous body, listening to her cry out his name. He ducked down for one final kiss before rising up and out of the bed.

His erection pressed against the confines of his boxers as he stood, jutting out loud and proud. He clenched his jaw and tugged the covers back over Wren, not missing the way her eyes tracked over him. "I'm gonna grab a cold shower," he said. "Rest, and then we'll have breakfast after you're ready and meet with my teammates. Tonight, we'll get your sister back."

***

Wren nervously swallowed as the men made preparations late that night. She didn't know half of what was going on, only that they'd move in and get Lily. Luke had been hunkered down for hours, going over building schematics and maps of the area and discussing the main players of the trafficking ring. Ava had been uncharacteristically silent for much of the day, but when Wren asked if she was okay, Ava hadn't wanted to talk about it.

The women had settled in at the hotel the guys were at, planning to wait for Lily and hopefully her friends. Wren had thought it would be easier for Lily not to return to the resort where Ethan Mongrove had held her. Of course, this was assuming that Lily wasn't in need of immediate medical attention. There was always a chance they'd have to get her to a hospital, that she wouldn't be able to immediately fly home.

Luke had sworn they had the resources for a medivac if necessary, and her stomach had dropped. She hated even imagining what her sister had gone through. Wren was a nervous wreck, and she wasn't even the one in danger. Luke and his teammates were risking their lives to get Lily. It may have been their job, but it was almost hard to imagine men like them even existed—guys who'd willingly face danger head on to help others. Would she be that brave if tasked to do so? She'd do anything for her sister, but what about for a complete stranger?

Luke moved toward her, looking dark and dangerous in black cargo pants and a snug-fitting black tee. Their gear was stashed in a car somewhere, and briefly, she wondered how they'd gotten guns, weapons, and whatnot into Mexico. Obviously, they deployed all over and were experienced in moving equipment and weapons. Wren was so out of her element, she hardly knew what to think.

"You okay?" Luke asked, his blue gaze far too assessing. Despite their heated kisses in bed that morning, they'd been apart most of the day. He needed to meet with his teammates, and she wasn't about to interrupt them.

"Good. Just nervous," she said, her gaze tracking over the conference room the men had set up.

"Hey," Luke said, lightly lifting her chin so she was looking at him. "We'll get her. Things are going to happen quickly from here on out, but we have a location. This is exactly why the team flew down to Cancun. I want you and Ava to stay here together at the hotel. I don't want to be worrying about your safety when we're breaching the building."

"Okay. We'll wait here."

"Promise me," he said, leveling her with a gaze.

Wren bit her lip but nodded.

"Hell," he muttered, his thumb sweeping over her bottom lip before he ducked down for a brief kiss. Butterflies filled her stomach, and she knew it was as much from her nerves as from Luke's touch. Wren could feel everyone's eyes on them, but no one commented. They all knew Luke had stayed with her last night. They probably assumed they'd had sex, and she felt herself flushing. She was a grown woman. Even if they had spent hours exploring one another's bodies, it was nobody else's business. It's not like she was a virgin. Things with Luke just felt different somehow. More. It was crazy to have met someone practically local to New York City in another country, but there it was. She'd literally walked up to the bar beside him at her resort, thousands of miles from home. Fate had a strange way of working sometimes.

"So, it's really just an old warehouse?" she asked, attempting to focus on the task at hand. Her nerves were getting the best of her, and she hated that she had to sit around the hotel waiting and wondering what was going on.

"It is. I'm not sure what else is in there. The warehouse has some living space, but we just don't know what else is being stored—weapons, drugs."

"People," Wren said with a shudder as Luke frowned. "And you're positive she's there."

"She's there," Luke said, his voice hard. "We got confirmation from the bug we planted. They didn't have time to move the girls to a nightclub during the commotion last night. We also learned that they put out a hit on Ethan Mongrove."

Wren's jaw dropped. "But isn't he back in the U.S. and in Federal custody?"

"He is, but they have connections back in the States. He destroyed their property and no doubt brought unwanted attention to their entire trafficking ring. The local police might've been willing to turn a blind eye, but the story is big. Michael, the Marine officer he targeted, flew back to the States with his family this morning. I understand that Mongrove is trying to railroad him, claiming he was involved in the entire thing. The guy's image is squeaky clean."

"God. So now he's trying to ruin the career of

another Marine in addition to destroying the lives of the girls he's trafficked? Ethan Mongrove is pure evil."

"He is," Luke agreed.

"Promise you'll call me as soon as you have Lily."

Luke nodded. "I will. She'll be scared, but it might help to hear a familiar voice. She might be panicking though, Wren. If she doesn't want to talk about what happened or say much, you'll have to wait until she's ready."

"I know," she said, swallowing again to hold back her tears.

Luke reached out, gently brushing his knuckles over her cheek. Even though he was about to head out on an op, her blood heated. There was something about his touch that both electrified and soothed her. "Be careful," she pleaded.

"Always am," he said, his eyes shifting as Sam flipped the laptop shut and stood.

"We ready to roll?" Sam asked. Nick rose as well, and Luke ducked down and kissed Wren before turning to his buddies. She could see Sam smirking, his eyes darting between the two of them, but he was smart enough not to comment.

"We're ready. Stay here," Luke ordered, turning to meet her gaze at the last statement. She could see the determination in his eyes, the tenseness in his posture. His body was practically pulsing, looking ready to spring into action. He'd been gentle with her but was now in warrior mode. The former Delta was ready to move out on a mission, and it would be the most important night of Wren's life.

Chapter 20

Luke watched the streets of Cancun pass by from the back of the SUV. Sam gripped the steering wheel, turning sharply as they made a last-minute detour. Nick was barking out directions to the warehouse, but an unexpected vehicle nearby had them circling the block. It was unlikely they were tied to the human traffickers, but the men weren't taking any chances. He glanced down at his watch, bracing as Sam took another sharp turn. Oh-three-hundred. Luke clicked on his mic, giving their boss an update. "We're almost there. We'll notify you when we have the package."

"Roger that," Jett replied. "Let me know when you have eyes on them. The Feds are eager to wrap this up since it's all over the news."

"Understood," Luke said. "Over."

They made a series of turns as Sam checked the rearview mirror, finally slowing the SUV down. "I think that was a false alarm. We don't have a tail."

"Pull a maneuver like that back in New York, and you'd have a line of police cars chasing after you," Nick quipped.

"Good ol' Mexico," Sam muttered. "Home of corrupt cops, cartels, and nonexistent traffic laws."

"Nah. It's not all bad," Nick said.

"It's not all good either."

Luke scanned the streets again, the crowded strip of nightclubs and bars disappearing behind them as they headed into a more industrial area. The warehouse Lily was being held in was nearly fifteen thousand square feet. It was large enough for commercial trucks to load and unload their cargo and included several smaller rooms. They'd gone over detailed layouts earlier, discussing alternate entry and exit points to both the building and property. Nothing but more warehouses surrounded it, and the team expected it to be quiet at this hour.

"ETA is five minutes," Nick said, watching the GPS navigation on his cell phone.

"Roger," Luke replied. "We're good on the plan?"

"I stay in the vehicle to keep watch and for a quick getaway," Sam confirmed. "You two move in and rescue the teenagers. I'll be on standby for backup if needed."

"Thankfully it's not guarded by many of those thugs at this hour," Nick muttered. "It seemed to be heavily fortified the days they were receiving shipments."

Luke clenched his rifle, his gaze narrowing. "Too bad the sat imagery couldn't show us what was in those trucks. Weapons? People? Those poor girls will be terrified when Nick and I burst in there. We only have space for Lily and her friends in the SUV. Any other victims will have to be set free but left there." He slid his night-vision goggles on and adjusted the Kevlar vest he was wearing, his heartbeat accelerating. A strange sense of calm washed over him, just like it always did before an op. He was in the zone, ready to take out the enemy and rescue any civilians. The world was full of evil men, and he didn't feel remorse at taking the lives of those who willingly harmed innocents.

"Duffle bag's in the back." Luke said. They'd brought spare clothes in case the girls were being held without suitable clothing. Wren had paled when he'd told her why they needed clothes. It wasn't a matter of life or death—clearly, they weren't about to freeze or develop hypothermia in Cancun. But it would give them a small degree of comfort. They might've been held naked or in skimpy clothing while in captivity, but they didn't need to be in that state of undress around Luke and his teammates. He and his friends would never harm them, but they didn't know that. Whatever they could do to make the teenagers feel more comfortable, they would.

"Got it. I'll park across the street as discussed, away from the lamplight," Sam said. "Hopefully whatever cameras they have won't immediately pick us up. West said he could try and jam the signal but wasn't positive about that."

"Why the hell not?" Nick questioned.

Sam lifted a shoulder. "Normally that would be a breeze for him. I'm not sure what the issue was. Could be he was busy dealing with something else."

"It doesn't matter," Luke said. "We'll be in and out before they even know we're there. I suspect we'll only encounter a few guards. If it were too heavily fortified, it would arouse suspicions. The Mexican cops might not care, but they don't want other criminals taking what's theirs."

Sam pulled up to the warehouse across the street, staying in the shadows. Aside from the security lights around the perimeter, it was dark inside. Luke frowned as he looked across the street to their target. "Left quadrant is lit up."

"The bedrooms are back there," Nick pointed out.

Luke's free hand fisted, his other still gripping the rifle. "I don't see anyone patrolling outside. We'll have to anticipate someone is up in the warehouse, despite the hour. There's no other reason for so many lights to be on. You ready to roll out?"

"Affirmative," Nick said. "We'll move around the perimeter as discussed, use bolt cutters to open the gate, and then breach the building from the west."

"I'll be here until you get your asses back," Sam said. "Comms are good, so I can track where you are inside the building."

"Then we're a go," Luke said, opening the back door of the SUV. He closed it silently, not wanting to alert anyone that they were there. A moment later, he and Nick were crouching down as they jogged along the metal fence surrounding the property. Opening the larger gate for vehicles might trigger an alarm, but he hoped they could access the lot through the smaller gate intended for personnel without anyone noticing.

"Bingo," Nick said as they rounded the back. "Look at that. The larger gate has sensors that monitor when it opens and closes. The trucks that roll up need to be buzzed in or have a sensor mounted inside granting them access. That small gate ten yards away doesn't have the same system. You can't buzz in and out, but it's also easier to break in from that point."

"Let's do it," Luke affirmed. His gaze swept the area as Nick grabbed his bolt cutters, easily cutting through the simple padlock and sliding both items into his rucksack. "It's not too secure," he commented.

"Easier for us that way."

"So it seems," he said with a frown. "You'd think they'd have more security in place."

"I don't think they ever intended to keep women here," Luke said. "If they're in the nightclubs, they can prostitute them for the night. They weren't expecting one of the clubs to literally go up in flames."

"There were too many casualties from that," Nick ground out. "Just another thing on Mongrove's long list of evildoings." He eased open the gate, the men stilling. No alarms were triggered, and they quietly crept through.

"I'm guessing this is more of a short-term storage area," Luke said. "They receive shipments of goods—whatever the hell that is—and then distribute them. It's too empty for large quantities of high-value goods to be stored here long term."

The men jogged across the asphalt, looking around for cameras. If they were spotted, they'd have minutes to get out of here. Sam could hold off some vehicles if backup arrived for the owners of the warehouse, but Luke knew the traffickers were well-connected and highly armed. The last thing they needed was the Mexican police showing up.

"We breached the gate," Luke said into his mic.

"Approaching the back doors."

"Roger that," came Sam's reply.

The lights were still on in the left quadrant of the building, and the men grew closer to the back door. Luke pulled a small tarp out, dropping it over the low-hanging surveillance camera. The men lifted their night-vision goggles. Nick already had a silencer on his sidearm, and after testing the door handle, shot out the deadbolt. He pulled the door open, and the men moved quietly inside. One guard was asleep in a chair, and Nick aimed his weapon and pulled the trigger. The man slumped over, and Luke and Nick moved down the hallway, their gazes sweeping the area.

"One tango down," Nick said over the headsets.

"Roger that. All is quiet out here," Sam replied.

"The cargo bays are in the front of the building. The smaller rooms—bedrooms—are back here. Six total," Luke said in a hushed tone.

"And they even left the light on for us," Nick quipped.

A woman's voice had Luke slowing his steps, and he heard a soft cry from one of the rooms up ahead as it sounded like someone was smacked. Luke aimed his rifle toward the room, quietly moving forward. He gestured to Nick, who fanned out beside him, his head swiveling back and forth. They paused a few feet from the doorway, listening to a woman pleading. The door was slightly ajar, the sounds of a woman softly crying clear. Luke held up a hand, counting down.

Three.

Two.

One.

The men burst into the room, weapons ready. A man with his pants down was rising off the bed as they stormed in, reaching for his own weapon. Nick took aim and shot him, watching the man fall to the ground. Luke's heartrate spiked as the young Mexican teenager shrieked in surprise. She was half-naked and sobbing, backing away from them on the bed.

"We won't hurt you," Luke said, his chest clenching as she tried to cover herself with the sheets. "Are their other girls here?" he questioned. She held up her hands to ward them off. "No English. No English." Luke's gaze swept the room as Nick moved to grab the trafficker's weapon. A thump sounded from the room next door. Luke cocked his head toward it. "Let's search the other rooms. She's not a threat."

The two men exited the room, scanning the hallway. The next door was locked. Not wasting any time, Nick aimed at the doorknob and shot. A female voice screamed in surprise as they stormed in. Luke's eyes swept over her. She was young, possibly another teenager, and she looked Mexican as well.

"We won't hurt you," Nick said. "Have you seen these girls?"

Luke pulled his phone from his pocket and swiped the screen, slowly approaching the trembling girl. "Do you speak English?" he asked.

"No. No English," she said, her voice shaking.

Luke held up his phone, showing her the picture of Lily. The girl's eyes widened. "Si," she said, nodding. "Si." She raised a hand, pointing to the doorway.

"She's here?" Luke asked.

The girl nodded again and pointed. "Si. Si."

Nick's gaze darted between the two of them. "Let's search the other rooms."

Leaving the teenager on the bed, Luke moved swiftly toward the door. The last room on the right wasn't locked. Luke gestured to his teammate, and then they moved in, aiming their rifles at the bed. A blonde teenager screamed in surprise, holding both hands up. She was dirty, her hair tangled, her clothes looking unwashed. She had on jeans and a tee shirt, something any American teenager might wear, and was barefoot.

"Lily Martin?" Luke asked as he lowered his weapon, his voice louder than he'd intended.

Her eyes widened, no doubt realizing he was American. "Y—yes. Who are you?" Her voice was hoarse, and his gaze tracked over her, looking for injuries.

"We're here to rescue you. We were tasked by the U.S. Government to fly down to Mexico and get you safely home. How many men are holding you here?"

Lily rubbed her hands across her thighs, a move he'd seen Wren do before. "In this building? I think only two. We were moved here last night. I was in a hotel the first few days," she said, her voice shaking. "Then I was held in a room at a club. There was some type of explosion last night."

"And they brought you here," Nick said.

"Yes. Me and several other girls. Wh—what happened to E? He wouldn't tell me his real name, but he's American. He's the man who took me."

"The man who kidnapped you has been arrested and is currently in U.S. custody," Luke explained. "He's not a threat to you anymore. Are you able to walk out of here on your own?"

Lily nodded and stood up, nearly stumbling. Nick moved closer. "Are you hurt?" he asked.

"No, just hungry and probably dehydrated."

"We'll get you water and food shortly," Luke assured her, moving to her side. She brushed her hair back, and he could tell she hadn't bathed in a while, which was almost a relief. Maybe they hadn't touched her yet. "Hold on to my arm," he instructed. "Are your friends being held here?"

"My friends?" she asked in confusion.

"A week after you were kidnapped, three of your friends disappeared as well."

"Oh my God," she whispered, faltering. Luke steadied her with a frown. "If they are here, I haven't seen them at all. I met a guy online, and he and I talked for a while. Chatted over private messages. It was stupid, but I agreed to let him pick me up at my parents' house. He wasn't who he said at all. He was old and in the military, I think. He'd promised me he'd get me into modeling and just—" She burst into tears. "I thought he was young, just a few years older than me. The pictures he posted weren't really him."

"It's all right. You're safe, and we'll get you out of here. He won't ever be able to hurt you again."

Luke exchanged a glance with Nick. "I'll search the remaining rooms," Nick said. "You get Lily to the SUV. I'll follow shortly."

"Think you're ready to hustle on out?" Luke asked. Lily looked up at him, the fear evident in her eyes. "I'll keep you safe," he promised. "One of our guys is waiting outside. Oh, and I have some good news. Your sister is here in Cancun. You can see her soon."

"Wren?" Lily asked, tears rolling down her cheeks.

Luke nodded. "She flew down here looking for

you. It's a long story, and I'm sure she'll tell you about some of it. Let's roll on out," he said, nodding toward the door. "We've got an SUV across the street and want to make a hasty exit. Wren and a friend of hers are back at the hotel. You can talk with her in the car if you like. I've got her number programmed into my phone. We'll get you back to the hotel, and you can see her for yourself. Once we make sure you're good to travel, we'll arrange a private jet to fly home. Wren can catch a ride with us, too. You'll be back in the States soon."

"Okay," she said, shakily walking down the hall at his side. "It's really over?"

"It's over," he assured her. "Let's get you home."

Chapter 21

Wren stood in her apartment a week later, her nerves getting the best of her. It had been a whirlwind seven days. She'd reunited with her sister at the hotel in Cancun, and they'd flown back home with Luke and his teammates on a private jet. Wren's reunion with her sister had been heartbreaking. Ethan Mongrove had held Lily captive at the resort, where he'd drugged and assaulted her. Lily told them that when Ethan had sold her to the traffickers, he'd claimed she was a virgin, and they'd been saving her for a special auction. As horrifying as the ordeal with Ethan had been, she hadn't been forced to spend night after night with multiple men. Still, the trauma she'd endured would take a long while to move forward from. Lily received medical attention once they'd landed in Pennsylvania and was in counseling. It would be a lengthy recovery, and after spending the week with her sister, Wren was finally back in New

York.

Her phone buzzed, and she grabbed it from her nightstand. She'd talked to Luke every night that week, and he was picking her up in Manhattan so they could finally get to the date he'd promised her.

Luke: *Can't wait to see you. I'll be there in thirty. Traffic is a bitch.*

Wren: *Now you know why I don't have a car.*

Luke: *Good choice. ;)*

Wren: *It was until I met a man who lives in the middle of nowhere.*

Luke: *Upstate isn't nowhere.*

Wren: *So says you. I need to finish getting ready. I'm only half dressed.*

Luke: *You won't get any complaints from me…*

Wren: *Hmmm. Maybe if you're good, you'll see me in a state of undress later.*

Luke: *I like the sound of that.*

Wren smiled as she set her phone back down. Even though they'd only spent one night together and shared nothing more than heated kisses, she still recalled waking up with Luke at her side. It hadn't felt awkward or uncomfortable. It felt…safe. He was sexy as hell, but she felt at peace with him. It made no sense to fall for a guy so quickly, but she'd always trusted her gut. They still had a lot to learn about one another, but she couldn't wait to see him.

She slipped into her dress and then tossed some things into her overnight bag. Luke had promised to take her to a little Italian restaurant near his home an hour north of the city. They'd have a delicious meal, drink some wine, and then relax at his place. Something about escaping the hustle and bustle of Manhattan just sounded right. She'd barely been back at her apartment, but ever since returning from her parents' home in Philly, she'd felt uneasy. It was silly. She'd lived alone for years. She was a grown woman. Lily's kidnapping had shaken her and set her on edge in a way she hadn't expected. Her sister was home. Safe. Still, Wren couldn't help but think it wasn't over. It didn't make sense given that Ethan Mongrove was in custody. The traffickers were thousands of miles away. A hint of anxiety crept over her, and she let out a shaky sigh.

Brushing those negative thoughts aside, she dropped a slinky little nightgown into her bag. It was similar to the one she'd brought to Cancun and made her feel feminine and sexy. The dress she had on now wasn't overly revealing but showed off her figure. Nervous butterflies filled her stomach as she stepped into her heels. When Luke knocked on her door half an hour later, she hurried to answer it. After undoing a series of locks, she pulled it open and smiled. Luke wasted no time, just strode in like he'd been there a million times and collected her in his arms for a searing kiss. They were both breathing heavily by the time they came up for air, Wren clinging to his biceps and inhaling his clean, woodsy scent.

"I've been waiting all week to do that," he said with a lazy grin. His hand on the small of her back felt good. Comforting. Her entire body pulsed with awareness now that he was here, and she felt herself flushing as his gaze raked over her.

"Me too. You smell good," she blurted out.

Luke chuckled, leaning closer once again and nuzzling her neck. His lips caressed her skin in a light kiss. Her breasts pressed against his muscular chest, and she felt her nipples harden. "So do you," he said huskily. "Still floral, but without the coconut scent from Mexico."

"That was my sunscreen," she giggled as he nuzzled her neck again.

Luke lifted his head, his blue eyes gleaming as he gazed at her. "You look great. I like this dress on you." The heat of his gaze was almost enough to send her up in flames.

"Thank you," she said, suddenly feeling shy.

Luke's eyes softened. "So are you all set? I made a reservation for seven, which should give us plenty of time."

"Yeah. Just let me grab my bag."

"Hell no. That's my job, sweetheart," he said, striding across the small studio to her bed. Luke grabbed the handles on her lavender duffle bag. It looked feminine in his big hand, and she felt herself flushing. He'd held her close a moment ago, but she was already imagining his hands running over her later. Luke had told her he had a guest room if she'd be more comfortable there, but she'd insisted that would be silly. He'd already stayed in her room in Mexico, holding her in his arms as they slept.

"Where'd you park?" she asked.

"In a garage down the block."

"Oh, I'm sorry. I should've come down to meet you so you didn't have to pay for parking."

"No way," he said, his gaze flicking over her again as his lips quirked. "I don't want you lugging everything down there yourself, and I don't mind. So, did you talk to your sister today?" he asked as he walked back toward her.

"Yeah. She sounded a little better. Don't get me wrong, I know she has a long road to recovery, but she sounded a tiny bit like her old self. She even laughed at something I said."

"That's great. It's good she has you and your parents for support. She's been through hell. It really makes me want to murder the guy who took her. He's got to go through due process and all that, but damn. Men like that aren't worth the uniform they wear."

"He disgusts me," she said. "I hope he rots in jail. You know, Lily mentioned some guy named 'Mick' when we were talking this week. I think she overheard Ethan talking to him? I'm not sure who he is though. I would've mentioned it sooner, but I was hoping she'd be able to tell me more. I didn't want to push her for more information before she's ready."

"Huh. I'll let the team know. The Feds are leading the investigation. Now that you mention it, Ethan did say something about a guy named Mick. He spewed out a ton of names as he was arrested, according to my teammates. I'm just glad they found the other missing teenagers unharmed."

"Me too," Wren said, crossing to the counter to grab her purse. "It's hard to believe they were here the entire time, being held in a basement outside Philly. Something's been bothering me about that. If Ethan was in Mexico with my sister, how were Lily's friends kidnapped a week later? He was posting photos from the resort the entire time."

"The FBI is investigating several possibilities. It turns out that one of Juan's men was in the States recently. Ethan had been communicating with Lily's friends online, but one theory is that Juan's guy was the person who took them. The man who picked up the other teenagers was disguised, and we don't have an accurate description of him. The girl who'd been in a coma remembers next to nothing. The other two were terrified and only could share bits and pieces of their ordeal. We don't have a description of the suspect."

Wren bit her lip, thinking. "Well, say Juan or some other accomplice took them. Why would he leave them in Philly?"

"Ethan had a short-term rental there. We assume if he couldn't get Lily out of the country immediately, he would've taken her there."

"Jesus," she murmured. "It's terrifying to know the types of evil people lurking out there in the world."

"It burns me up," Luke said. "That's part of the reason why once the guys and I left the service, we joined Jett's company. I'll never be the type of man who can sit at a desk all day. I need to be physically active. And helping people? Ridding the world of evil?" He shrugged. "It was a no-brainer."

"You're braver than I'll ever be," she admitted.

Luke burst into laughter, looking at her in disbelief. "You flew to Mexico alone to track down Lily. That's brave as hell, sweetheart."

"I guess."

"You guess," he jokingly scoffed. "Woman. You're killing me."

Wren giggled as Luke smiled at her, his hand gently wrapping around the nape of her neck as he gave her a kiss. Her hands landed on his muscled chest, and she could feel the strength of him. Being with Luke always made her feel safe. Secure. "Should we get going? The Italian place is amazing. The owners used to live in the city but escaped the craziness to head upstate."

"It sounds perfect. Let me just grab my keys to lock up."

Chapter 22

Luke drove Wren back to his house after dinner, his hand resting on her thigh. They'd talked and flirted throughout the meal, and he'd stolen a quick kiss, enjoying the flush that had spread across her cheeks. While they'd shared a few meals in Mexico together, her sister's kidnapping had been on the forefront of everyone's minds. It was work, not a vacation. Tonight was different.

"I talked to Sam earlier," Luke commented as he drove along the dark road, the music in his SUV turned down low.

"Oh yeah? How's he doing?"

"He was wondering if Ava blocked his number. It sounds like he'd saved her texts even though he never responded after their night together in Paris. He tried to get in touch with her after we returned from Cancun but hasn't heard back."

Wren lifted a shoulder, her hair shifting with the movement as Luke glanced over. She was gorgeous in the dim light, and he couldn't wait to have more time alone together tonight. "I don't think she really wants to talk to him," Wren admitted.

"Yeah. I kind of got that on the plane ride home," he said.

Wren shook her head. "Yeah. I think we all got that impression. Ava reached out several times after she got home from France and never heard back from Sam. It stung."

"I don't know what the deal was with him. I think he's regretting it now. He had told us about the night he spent in Paris with a woman."

Luke chuckled as Wren's jaw dropped. "Seriously?"

"Nothing salacious," Luke quickly added. "Well, not too salacious. I chalked it up to a vacation fling. I'm guessing he never expected to see her again."

"Then why pretend he would? That was a dick move. At any rate, he had his chance. She texted and called, and he blew her off. Life moves on."

"Is she dating someone?"

"Ava? No, but don't go getting any ideas. We're not playing matchmaker."

Luke's lips quirked. "No way. I don't think I'm really the matchmaker type, and Sam's a big boy. If he wants to see Ava again, it sounds like he'll have a lot of groveling to do." Luke flipped on the turn signal, heading into his neighborhood. "This is my street. I've got a small place," he added as they passed several houses. "It's got a decent-sized yard though and is plenty of room for me."

"It can't be smaller than my studio," she pointed out.

"Well, you got me there," he said with a chuckle.

"I just didn't want you expecting some huge house."

"I didn't know what to expect," she admitted. "I'm just happy to be with you."

Luke gave her a quick glance, squeezing her thigh. "Me too."

He pulled into his driveway a minute later, telling Wren to stay put. He rounded the vehicle and opened the passenger door, his gaze raking over her. The dress Wren had on clung to her perfect curves, showcasing her breasts and hips. He reached in and undid the seatbelt for her, taking his time as he leaned close. Luke took her hand, helping her to step down from his SUV. Wren in those sexy heels was making his dick twitch. He couldn't help imagining her in those and nothing else, her shapely legs and feminine curves displayed to perfection. If he didn't have neighbors and they were further along in their relationship, he'd be tempted to turn her around right now and press her against his SUV. Luke would love to hike up that clingy dress and pull her panties aside, caressing her intimately before sinking into her silken folds.

"I'll grab your bag from the back," he said, clearing his throat. He didn't release her hand, his thumb soothing over her skin, and she stepped even closer. Wren's floral scent surrounded him, so feminine and soft. He popped the back hatch and grabbed her duffle, pushing the button for it to automatically close.

"Let's go inside," he said, nodding to the front door. "I'll show you around, and then we can have a drink and sit and relax."

"That sounds perfect."

Luke couldn't resist ducking for a quick kiss before

he led her inside. The idea of Wren in his space made him want to roar in approval. And her in his bed? He'd offered the guestroom if she felt more comfortable, but the idea of her lush body against his all night sent his libido rising. She was sexy and sweet, and Luke loved the idea of holding her close and waking up with her in his arms.

Several hours later, Wren was snuggled up beside Luke on his back patio. They'd talked and simply enjoyed the quiet time together, Wren sipping on another glass of wine while Luke nursed his beer. "I still can't get over how many stars you can see out here," she said, a smile playing about her lips.

"Living in the city is different from upstate, but I wouldn't change it for the world. I saw a lot of different places in the military, traveled everywhere, but this just feels like home."

"Where are you originally from?" she asked.

"Connecticut. My parents still live there. I think they wish I'd move back," he said with a quiet laugh. "They understand my commitment to the job though. They've met Jett and my teammates at various points over the years. They're all good guys. We might not be in uniform anymore, but the work we do is important."

"You'll get no arguments from me. Lily literally owes you her life. If you hadn't found her—" Wren's voice cut off as she shuddered, and Luke tightened his arms around her.

"It's in the past now. That asshole will be in jail, dishonorably discharged from the military. Lily is young, and I know she's got a long road ahead as far as recovery, but she's strong as hell."

"She is. I just hope she knows not to chat with

strange men online anymore, or worse, meet them in person."

"It was a tough lesson to learn. She's not the first girl we've rescued and won't be the last. It never gets easier, but I'm happy as hell if we can reunite someone with their family. Same with my teammates. It's hard, but we can see the good we're doing."

"So only two of your teammates have girlfriends?" Wren asked.

"Why, are you looking to meet someone?" Luke joked.

Wren playfully swatted at him. "I happen to have recently met a man down in Mexico, thank you very much."

His lips brushed against the top of her head as he huffed out a laugh. "Thank goodness for that. And yeah, two of the guys are engaged. It happened kind of quickly for both of them, but when you know, you know. Jett's fiancée used to live in Manhattan," he commented.

"Oh yeah? How'd they meet?"

"He was in the city for meetings and met her at a bar. It sounds cliché, but it's true. Anna went home with him for the night, and the rest is history. She basically moved in and never left."

"Wow. I'm not sure I'd ever be quite that impulsive," Wren said.

"That's Anna for you," Luke said with a laugh. "You'll meet her sometime." He watched as Wren sleepily blinked up at the stars, stifling a yawn. "You look tired. Maybe we should get ready for bed. There's a great diner near here where we can have brunch tomorrow, or I can cook breakfast for you if you prefer."

"Hmmm. Can we decide tomorrow?"

"Sure thing," he said easily. "So what do you think? Should we head in?" His fingers trailed over her arm, and Luke didn't miss the way she shivered at his touch.

"Yeah. Probably. It's awfully comfy out here," she said, squeezing him gently. He glanced down, looking at her slender arm wrapped around his waist. Somehow, they'd ended up on the same chaise lounge, Wren leaning against him like she was exactly where she belonged. The thought was somewhat startling. He'd never needed a woman before, but it was already hard to imagine life without this one.

"You can snuggle up next to me in bed," he promised, helping her to sit upright. His hands gripped her waist as he helped her to stand, and then Luke rose as well, towering above her from behind. His arm snaked around her waist, and he pulled her close, dropping a kiss on the top of her head. "Maybe it makes me sound like a caveman, but I kind of love the idea of you in my space, in my bed."

"A caveman, huh?" she asked with a laugh as he released her. "You're more like Batman than a caveman with all the people you save and bad guys you go after. Show me your bat cave," she teased.

"Will do," he said with a wink. He grabbed her empty wineglass along with his beer bottle and guided her back inside his home. Luke double-checked the locks, closing the blinds afterward. "I've got a security system, too," he explained. "It's a safe area, but I'm always cautious."

"Well, you saw all the locks on my place," Wren said. "City life, you know? You can't be too careful."

Luke nodded, not liking that life in the city could

necessitate something like that. Wren was a grown woman though. He had absolutely no say in where she lived or what she did. He grabbed her bag from where he'd left it in the living room and gestured for her to proceed him down the hall. "I gave you the quick tour earlier, but my room's the last on the left."

"Got it," she said, turning to smile back at him. She'd ditched her heels hours ago but still looked sexy as hell in the dress she wore. The fabric crisscrossed over her breasts enticingly, and the necklace she wore dangled down near her cleavage.

"Why don't you get ready first," he said as they walked into the bedroom, nodding toward the bathroom. His phone buzzed, and he frowned as he pulled it from his pocket and read the text from Jett.

"Is everything okay?" she asked, looking worried.

"Yep. Just more stuff they're dealing with involving Mongrove. We don't need to worry about it tonight. Go ahead and do whatever you need to do. Where do you want this?" he asked, lifting her bag.

"Um, I'll take it I guess." She grabbed it from him with two hands and disappeared into his bathroom, the door snicking shut behind her. His gaze tracked across the bedroom. His room was neat if not somewhat bare. Luke wasn't much into decorating and was fine with the basics. He couldn't help but wonder what Wren thought of his utilitarian space. Luke had learned to live with little while in the Army, but he wanted her to feel at home. Her studio was small but looked modern and sleek, with several personalized touches.

He quickly thumbed a response back to his boss, setting his phone on the nightstand. He could hear the water running as Wren got ready and scrubbed a hand over his jaw. He'd love to slowly undress her, exploring every inch of her body, but he was more concerned in making sure she was comfortable tonight. Luke was more than fine with taking things at her pace. If that meant simply holding her, he'd enjoy the feel of her in his arms, her body pressed up against his.

Luke stilled as Wren emerged from the bathroom a few minutes later. She'd tied her silky robe over the pajamas he assumed she wore underneath, but nothing disguised her creamy skin or perfect curves. The satin of her robe crisscrossed over her breasts and hit mid-thigh, her toned legs peeking out beneath. She was fresh-faced, the light makeup she wore washed off, but still the prettiest damn thing he'd ever seen. The slight vulnerability that crossed her face made his protective instincts rise. Once again, he couldn't help but reassure her. "Are you sure this is okay? I can crash in the guestroom if you'd like. You can take my bed."

"What? Don't be silly. You stayed in my room in Mexico. I want you here with me."

"All right," he said, his voice husky. "Let me quick get ready." He moved toward the bathroom before he did something crazy, like pull her onto the bed and kiss every curve of her body. He brushed his teeth and relieved himself, moving back into the bedroom a few minutes later. Wren was already under the covers, her robe draped over the chair, looking a little tired but still sweet as hell. He sank to the edge of the bed, taking off his shoes.

Luke stood and undid his pants, pushing them down his muscled legs. He felt Wren's eyes on him, the attraction in hers as he turned back around enough to make his blood heat. He left his tee shirt and boxers on, not wanting Wren to feel uncomfortable, and she lifted the sheets. The sexy little nightgown she had on clung to her curves, and he felt his cock stiffening. It was the same style as the one she'd worn in Cancun, and memories of her body pinned beneath his filled his mind. He'd hated leaving her in bed the morning after he'd spent the night. Their brief make-out session before he'd reluctantly climbed out of bed had left him hard as a rock. She'd been scared that night in Mexico, and the trust she had in him to keep watch over her was humbling. Holding her close hadn't been a hardship.

Luke slid into bed beside her, reaching over to turn off the light.

"Is this okay?" he confirmed.

"More than okay," she said, snuggling against him with a yawn.

Wren's slender arm wrapped around his waist, her head resting against his shoulder as he pulled her close. Her bare legs tangled with his made his dick twitch, and Luke couldn't stop the smile that spread across his face. Had he ever wanted to simply hold a woman before? Doubtful.

"I like having you here," he said, his voice gruff.

"Me too. Plus, I feel safer with you than at my place."

He frowned. "You don't like your studio?"

"I never minded it before. I've just felt on edge since getting back from Mexico—not tonight," she hastily added. "Just when I'm alone. It's hard to explain. I've lived by myself for years, but Lily's kidnapping shook me. I feel like I'm always looking over my shoulder now, expecting something bad to happen."

"That's completely normal," he said in a low voice, squeezing her gently. "But hey, you're a journalist, right? I assume you can work remotely sometimes. You can stay here whenever you want. We'll get to spend time together, and you won't be in your studio alone."

"What if you're gone?" she questioned. "You guys travel a lot."

"Hey," he said, tilting her face up. Their eyes met in the darkness, and his thumb briefly skimmed over her lower lip. "I don't mind if you want to stay here. I like that you feel comfortable. We don't know everything about each other yet, but I know for a fact that I've never felt this way before. I've never wanted to wake up next to a woman, to be in a relationship. That's because I was with the wrong women. I hadn't met you. You're smart and beautiful, sexy, gutsy, and you make me laugh. I'd be crazy to let you get away."

Her lips parted in surprise, and he ducked down for a tender kiss. Wren melted against him, letting Luke take control as his hand moved to the back of her head, his fingers tangling in her hair. Luke's tongue slid inside her mouth, moving against hers. The air between them grew thicker, Wren's breasts rising and falling against his chest. His own heart was pounding, adrenaline pumping through his veins. His cock swelled, and Luke was certain she could feel it pressing against her.

Luke's free hand roamed over her. His fingers skimmed along the side of one breast, down to her waist, then cupped her ass, hitching her slightly higher as he claimed her mouth. Wren whimpered but submitted to him, letting Luke remain in control.

Without thought, he rolled them both over, his large body hovering above her own. He kissed her again in the darkness, tasting the mint of her toothpaste and the sweetness that was pure Wren. Her breasts rose and fell, pushing against the soft fabric of her nightgown, her nipples pebbled.

"Tell me to stop," he rasped, his lips grazing along the column of her neck. He lightly nipped at her, sucking on the tender skin. Wren let out a gasp, tilting her head to give him better access. She whimpered, pulling him closer, her thighs parting as he settled between her legs.

"I don't want you to stop," she protested.

"Wren." His lips moved down her neck. Kissing. Sucking. Wren's floral scent was driving him crazy, and his cock pressed against the confines of his boxers, his erection flush against her core. Luke shifted and kissed his way down to her cleavage, one large hand palming her breast. His thumb rubbed over her peaked nipple through the fabric, and he smiled at the tiny gasp she made. "You're perfect," he murmured. "So sexy and sweet." His fingers trailed down one strap of her nightgown, so delicate beneath his big hand, and he pushed it off her shoulder. He lifted her breast free from the material, palming it gently before sucking her nipple into his mouth.

Wren arched up against him, letting Luke feast on her. He kneaded her flesh as he sucked on her breast, loving the way she squirmed beneath him. His tongue flickered over her nipple, and she clutched onto his biceps, crying out, her hips inadvertently bucking against him. Luke released her breast with a pop, moving to give the other the same attention. He shifted her nightgown once more, baring her other breast to him. Her chest was heaving, her breath coming out in tiny pants. Luke circled her areola with his tongue, teasing her. He planted kisses all over her breast, his stubble rubbing against her flesh. Wren was panting and clinging to him, and Luke smiled against her, ready to drive Wren out of her mind. He tongued her nipple, listening to her gasp.

Luke shifted slightly, and as his fingers skimmed up her thigh, he didn't miss the tiny moan she made as he got closer to her core.

"Hell. You're not wearing panties," he said gruffly, his large hand splaying over her lower belly as he pushed her skimpy nightgown up. His thumb trailed up her slit as she whimpered beneath him. Wren was neatly trimmed down below. Drenched. Perfect. "You're so wet, honey," he said, his voice thick with desire. "So ready for me."

"Luke," she pleaded.

"I got you," he rumbled.

He slid his thumb between her folds, feeling the silken arousal. She made a choking sound as he moved upward, circling her clit with the pad of his thumb. Luke shifted his hand and slid two fingers between her folds, playing with her gently for a moment before easing them inside her molten channel. Her inner walls clamped down around him, and he continued strumming her clit with his thumb. He kissed her, hard, stealing her breath and swallowing her cries. As Wren threw her hands above her head, landing on the pillow, Luke took them in his own, holding her in place.

He pumped his fingers in and out, loving how slick and aroused she was for him. The covers on the bed had been pushed off, and with her breasts spilling out above her nightgown, her pussy bared to him, Wren was his for the taking. He moved his hand faster, circling her swollen bud. She was getting closer, bucking her hips up toward him, getting tighter around his fingers. Luke didn't let up, and as he pressed down on her clit, she exploded, crying out his name into the night.

He gentled his kisses, slowing the movements of his hand as he brought her back down. Wren's legs were spread wide for him, and she was so sexy and vulnerable in that moment, letting him pleasure her, it made his breath catch.

"I want you inside me," she panted a moment later, still gasping for breath.

"Are you sure?" he questioned, nuzzling against her neck and placing a tender kiss just beneath her ear. He pulled his hand free from her swollen sex, lifting his fingers to his mouth to suck off her juices. "God damn, you're sweet," he muttered. "I want to taste all of you later. Explore every inch."

Wren was already reaching between them, gripping his cock over his boxers. "Luke. I'm sure. Now."

He chuckled but lifted himself off her, pulling open the drawer of his nightstand to grab a condom. He stripped off his tee shirt and then carefully eased his boxers over his erection before shoving them down his legs and sheathing himself with the rubber.

"You're big," she murmured, catching a glimpse of him in the dim light.

"I'm yours," he said, climbing back onto the bed and leaning down for a kiss. His erection pressed against her leg as he moved, and her small hand circled him, pumping once. Twice. Luke muttered an oath. "I'm not going to be able to last if you keep that up."

"Then get inside me already," she said. Luke claimed her sassy mouth in a kiss, lining himself up with her center. Her thighs were spread wide, and Wren was already lifting her hips toward him. He notched himself at her center and pushed inside, her swollen walls clamping down around him. Luke stilled, shocked at the rightness of being inside her, of her pussy squeezing his cock like he was exactly where he belonged.

Wren huffed out a tiny gasp as he bottomed out, her breasts pushing against his chest, her legs trembling.

"Are you okay?"

"Perfect. I just—you're perfect."

He ducked down and kissed her once, his erection stroking her inner walls. "I want to see you," he said. She shifted beneath him, reaching over to turn on the nightstand light with Luke still buried inside her welcoming body. Dark eyes blinked and then met his, her cheeks flushed, her hair tousled, her lips swollen from his kisses. His eyes raked down over Wren's body, taking in her pretty pink nipples and full, plump breasts. Unable to resist, he trailed his hand down, squeezing one gently. His thumb skimmed over her nipple, teasing her. His eyes tracked lower to where their bodies joined. Wren's gaze landed there as well, her eyes wide. Luke was big and thick, and she took him perfectly.

"I can't hold still any longer," he ground out, his erection throbbing inside her.

"Then take me. Please," she begged.

Luke shifted back, pulling her ass up onto his thighs. Her back was on the mattress, her bottom in his lap, and her legs spread wide around his waist. She gasped at the sudden change in position, but he could enjoy all of her this way. Watch as his cock slowly sank into her body. Gaze at her breasts as they bounced with his every thrust. Stare into her eyes. She arched back, throwing her hands over her head again as Luke began to move. He had the random thought of tying those slender wrists to the headboard. Something about having Wren at his complete and utter mercy made him want to roar in approval. She gripped the headboard anyway, desperate for something to hold onto, and Luke's hands tightened around her hips. She was his.

He thrust into her, listening to her pants and whimpers as he set the pace. Watching the pools of desire in her eyes.

"I want you to come again for me," he said, his voice gravel. He thrust again, his cock swelling even more.

"Oh God. I can't," she panted, a flush spreading from her cheeks down to her chest.

"You can." He thrust harder, faster as she cried out, her breasts jiggling with the movement. Luke slid one hand to her pussy, toying with her clit. "Come for me, sweetheart. Let me hear you crying out for me again. I love my name on your lips."

She gasped as he bucked into her again and again and pressed down on her clit like he'd done before. Her pussy spasmed around him, her legs shaking, and then she cried out his name, arching off the bed as she tumbled over the precipice, stealing his heart as she surrendered to him. He could feel her inner walls pulsing around him, nearly causing him to explode as well. He needed to be closer, consuming all of her.

Luke rose to his knees and prowled over her, one hand sliding under her ass to hold her in place, his other arm sliding beneath her back, his hand at her nape. He buried his face in her neck and thrust harder, muttering an oath as his balls tightened. Wren's fingernails raked down his back, her legs wrapped tight around him, and he could still feel her pussy spasming around his dick, her sweet cries of pleasure spurring him on. He thrust one last time and exploded, Wren clinging to him as he muttered her name.

She was flushed beneath him, a thin sheen of sweat coating both their bodies, and he kissed her again, still buried balls deep inside his woman. Wren was his. There was no doubt in his mind. He couldn't imagine ever bringing another woman into his bed, his life, or his heart.

Chapter 23

Wren shifted in bed the next morning, flushing as her bare breasts pressed against Luke's chest. They were both naked and tangled between the sheets, and she was deliciously sore from their lovemaking. After taking her the first time, Luke had rolled over and pulled her on top. She'd seated herself atop Luke and then rode him slowly, Luke helping to guide her movements with those big hands of his gripping her hips. She could tell he'd loved watching her above him, her breasts bouncing each time he thrust upwards and simultaneously pulled her down on his cock. Luke was big and thick, and each time she'd sunk down, the base of his erection had rubbed against her clit, sending sparks of pure pleasure shooting through her. Luke had been in complete control, taking her how he'd wanted, and she'd shattered once more, collapsing in his arms as she'd cried out his name.

The sun peeking in from the slats on the blinds

danced across the bed, and she stifled a yawn. Wren adjusted one leg, feeling the hair on Luke's muscular thigh tickle her skin. His hard body was in complete contrast to her own softness and curves, but she loved how safe she felt with him.

Luke stirred, his hand running over her bare back. "Morning," he mumbled, his voice gruff.

"Morning," she said softly, glancing up at him.

"How'd you sleep?" he asked, his eyes still closed.

"Good. Great actually. Someone might've worn me out."

His lips quirked as he opened his eyes. "I can't seem to keep my hands to myself around you. Last night was amazing." His hands raked over her, landing on her bare bottom. He squeezed her cheeks gently, possessively, and she felt arousal pool at her core. Luke had made her come readily and easily last night. She'd always enjoyed sex, but with him? It felt like something else entirely. He'd commanded her body as they'd made love, his hands and mouth everywhere, and she'd loved every second of it.

"It was," she agreed. She pressed a kiss to his chest, loving how relaxed and easy things felt between them.

His fingers trailed lower, teasing right where the curve of her ass met her thigh. She squirmed against him, and she sensed rather than saw his smile. Luke loved to tease and pleasure her, and he'd made her come more times than she could count. "I loved hearing you cry out my name last night," he said huskily. She flushed as he chuckled. "What, you're getting shy on me now?" he teased. "I've got that image of you naked and riding me burned into my brain forever."

"Oh stop. You do not."

Luke lifted the sheets to sneak a peek, winking at her. "Just confirming. Yep. Same picture I have in my head. Gorgeous breasts. Pretty pink nipples. Killer curves. You're smart and sweet but sexy as hell, too. And I love the way you blush around me. I feel like I know some big secret—exactly how to drive you wild."

"Luke," she said, her voice breathless.

"I'm going to taste you," he said, rolling them both over and lazily grinning down at her. "We never made it that far last night." And then he kissed his way down her body, across her flat stomach, before settling between her thighs. His thumb trailed up her slit as his eyes darkened. Then he was tossing her legs over his broad shoulders, pressing closer, and proceeding to drive her out of her mind.

*****

After another round of lovemaking in the shower, where Luke had taken her against the wall, slow and sweet as the steam surrounded them, they finally made it to brunch. The heated looks he kept shooting at her from across the cozy booth were about to drive her out of her mind.

"What?" she asked with a smile, taking a sip of her coffee.

"I like this," he said with a grin. "You. Me. Brunch. I think we should make a habit of you staying over more."

"You'll get no arguments from me," she agreed, smiling back at him before looking around the diner. It was busy with the weekend rush, and she was glad they'd snagged a table without needing to wait. Her eyes tracked over a few people before she noticed a tall man with broad shoulders hovering near the doorway. He locked eyes with Wren for a beat before turning, shoving the door open and striding quickly across the parking lot.

Luke caught her frown, looking concerned. "What's wrong?"

"Nothing. I just saw some guy looking at me. He's already leaving. I'm just paranoid now," she said, shaking her head.

Luke followed her gaze to the parking lot, watching through the window as the man walked away. He had short, dark hair and a small bald spot at the back. He ducked into a SUV, closing the door behind him.

"I'm sure it's nothing," Wren said as she looked back to Luke, but she was clutching her coffee mug more tightly than before.

"Ethan Mongrove is behind bars," Luke assured her. "That wasn't him."

"I know. The entire situation just bothers me," she said. "Someone took Lily's friends. Why wasn't the second person caught yet?"

"That's what Jett was texting me about last night," Luke admitted. "They're coming up with nothing but dead ends so far. Mongrove still insists Michael O'Donnell was involved, but the guy's squeaky clean. He's serving in a position Mongrove wanted, so it sounds like a case of sour grapes. Ethan's pissed he didn't get the job, amongst other things. Most likely, it was one of Juan's men who kidnapped the other girls."

"Ethan's mad about a job he didn't get? That's

just…." Wren trailed off, shaking her head. "I don't know what it is. I've been researching him. Looking into all his friends on social media, trying to dig up the dirt. Someone's still out there who was involved in this. It freaks me the hell out."

Luke was watching her intently, and he reached across the table, taking her hand. "They'll find the guy and whoever else is involved. It's only a matter of time."

The waitress came over, setting steaming plates of food in front of each of them. Wren stared down at her vegetable omelet, a strange sense of foreboding washing over her. She was fine. She was safe. Luke was right here, and she knew he would never let anything happen to her. Still, she couldn't shake the feeling that something was coming—that the other shoe was going to drop, and she wouldn't be able to do anything to stop it.

Chapter 24

The next three weeks passed by in a blur. Luke and Wren spoke nearly every night, both by phone and video chat. They texted throughout the day, always remaining in touch. The guys had been sent out on a brief op but were home in a matter of days. Luke couldn't tell her where he'd gone, and she'd been even more on edge until she heard his deep, soothing voice once again. They'd spent several more weekends together, Luke crashing at her studio and taking Wren back to his house as well. She'd found that she much preferred the safety and serenity of his place. The bustling city had always appealed to her in the past, but now she enjoyed the quiet time alone upstate with Luke.

Lily was still in counseling but doing better than anyone had expected, and Wren talked with her most days. Lily's friends still remembered few details about the man who'd taken them, and Wren had tried to move on with her life. She'd dug around more into

Ethan Mongrove's family and friends, but she wasn't any further along than the authorities. Someone was out there who'd kidnapped the teenagers, but for the moment, the person was walking around a free man. Life went on anyway though, and Wren tried her hardest to move forward.

Her phone buzzed, and she glanced down at the text, a smile spreading across her face.

Luke: *Can't wait to see you tonight, honey.*

Luke: *Promise me you'll pack that red lacy thing.*

Wren giggled, flushing as she recalled the lace teddy she'd worn last weekend. Luke had pinned her beneath him, pulled the crotch aside, and pleasured her with his fingers and tongue. He seemed to love making her come apart in his arms, and she had absolutely no complaints about that.

Wren: *Maybe I have some new, sexy lingerie to bring.*

Luke: *Bring it all. ;)*

She laughed, thumbing another flirty reply.

Wren: *I thought you liked me naked best.*

Luke: *True. But you're underestimating how much I love undressing you.*

Wren: *I'll see what I can do. xoxo*

Her cheeks were flushed with excitement as she finished packing her bag. While they enjoyed their time together out of the bedroom, exploring his town or the city and just being together, their nights together were scorching. It was hard to believe that meeting a stranger in Mexico had changed her entire life. Luke was protective and more macho than the guys she'd dated in the past, but she felt comfortable with him in a way she couldn't even put into words. He made her feel both cherished and safe. It was too soon to even think about the "L" word, but she was falling for him hard.

A knock on her door thirty minutes later had her frowning in confusion. Luke wasn't supposed to be here until tonight, and she wasn't expecting anyone else. Wren peered through the peephole, spotting a middle-aged man standing outside. He was tall and clean cut, but uneasiness washed over her. She didn't recognize him as anyone who lived in her building, but somehow, he'd gotten past the doorman. Still, there was something she couldn't quite place—a familiarity that made her think she'd seen him somewhere before.

Wren unlocked her deadbolt and second lock but left the chain on, pulling the door open. "Can I help you?" she asked brusquely.

Piercing blue eyes gazed down at her. "Wren Martin?" he asked. "I'm Michael O'Donnell. I worked with the man accused of kidnapping your sister and was wondering if I might have a minute of your time."

"What's this about?"

"I worked with Ethan Mongrove for years. I understand the FBI has taken the lead on interviewing the victims, but we're doing our own internal investigation. NCIS is involved, and I've been in Pennsylvania and New York speaking with a few people about the case."

"You worked with Ethan?"

"Yes, ma'am. Unfortunately, he wasn't what he seemed. I had the displeasure of packing the things in his office after he was arrested. I found a large number of photographs. I was wondering if you'd be able to confirm the identity of Lily and her friends? I'll pass along the information to NCIS."

Wren frowned, biting her lip. "Can't the police do that? They have all their photos and information and could certainly ID them."

"Yes, but given you know them firsthand, this will be faster. It'll just be a minute of your time."

A neighbor came out of their apartment down the hall, and Michael turned at the sound, watching them walk away. The footsteps grew fainter, and suddenly, Wren froze. She recognized Michael from the back— broad shoulders, short cropped hair, and a small bald spot at the center of his head. She'd seen him in the diner weeks ago. He'd been following her then and was on her doorstep now.

"Sorry, I can't help you," she said, starting to close the door.

He turned back toward her, anger flashing across his features, and shoved the entire door with his body. Wren shrieked and jumped back, then tried to push the door shut so she could lock it. She opened her mouth to scream, and he sprayed something in her face through the crack in the door. Dizziness overtook her, and she stumbled back, weakly crying out for help. Wren fell to the floor, unable to control her movements, and the door was shoved all the way open, the chain breaking free from the force.

"Luke," she murmured weakly. "Luke's coming."

Rough hands grabbed her, yanking her up. "You'll never see that fucking asshole again," he spat out. "You're coming with me, princess." Wren tried to fight but instead fell against him as everything faded to black.

***

"What are you smiling about, buddy?" Sam asked knowingly as he strode into the reception area of Shadow Security Headquarters that afternoon. He snagged a glazed donut from the box on the counter, taking a bite. "Umm. Sweet. Kind of reminds me of—"

"Don't say it," Jett said as he walked by, knocking on the top of the counter to get Sam's attention.

"No worries, boss," Sam said with a grin as Jett continued on his way.

"Jesus. Enough with the sex talk," Luke muttered. "You were going on and on earlier about whatever woman you slept with last."

"Sweetest pussy ever," Sam agreed, watching as the door swung closed behind Jett as he moved into the secure area of the building.

Luke rolled his eyes. "Who's the lucky lady?"

"Ah, I'd never kiss and tell," Sam said, polishing off the rest of the donut.

"Bullshit," Nick said from where he stood, flipping through a magazine about guns. "Nice. Look at that one." He held up the page for his buddies to see.

Luke looked over and then glanced back at Sam. "To answer your question, I'm picking up Wren later on. She's coming to my place for the weekend."

"Things are getting serious between you two," Nick said with a grin. "Hell. Another one bites the dust. Guess ole Sam and I are on our own to hit up the bars. Gray usually doesn't want to come along."

"Can you blame him?" Luke joked. "He probably has better luck picking up women without you two assholes joining him."

Sam chortled, holding his hands to his chest. "Ouch. I'm wounded."

Luke pulled his phone from his pocket as it buzzed, wondering if Wren was texting him again. He'd teased her earlier about packing sexy lingerie for the weekend. Things between them were good. They had fun together and laughed. They enjoyed dinners out just as much as cooking a meal together or snuggling up on the sofa for a movie. And the nights? Hell. He wasn't sure he'd ever met a woman as compatible with him in bed. Luke enjoyed taking control and Wren seemed to come alive under his touch.

He frowned as he realized the text was from his boss.

Jett: *Just had an urgent update on Mongrove. Emergency meeting ASAP.*

"Shit," Sam said, brushing off his hands. "What the hell did that asshole do now?"

"Guess we'll find out," Luke muttered. He grabbed his badge as they moved to the secure area, holding it up to the sensor to access the back. He shoved the heavy door open, his teammates following as they moved down the hall.

Gray came jogging up behind them, covered in sweat. "What the hell's going on? I thought our briefing about the next op was in an hour. I was in the middle of a workout."

"It's something about Ethan Mongrove," Luke said, scrubbing a hand over his jaw. "Not sure what happened, but I've got a feeling the shit's about to hit the fan." They moved into the conference room, Jett and Ford already there.

"What's going on, boss?" Nick asked, yanking back a chair and sinking down into it.

"Someone offed Ethan Mongrove this afternoon,"

Jett said in a clipped tone.

"What?" Luke barked out, jaw dropping in surprise.

"The MPs were guarding him. Apparently, a high-ranking Marine demanded they allow him to meet with Ethan. They brought him to a secure room, where he was slipped something."

"Who was the Marine?" Gray asked.

"Michael O'Donnell. The same man Ethan targeted at the nightclub in Cancun. They were secretly working together until Ethan turned on him." Jett typed something into the laptop, pulling up the footage of the authorities questioning him several days ago. Two Federal agents were seated across from him, Ethan in an orange prison jumpsuit. Jett turned up the volume, the men watching in confusion.

"He's clean," one agent said. "Michael O'Donnell doesn't have any social media accounts. He's got an alibi for the day the girls disappeared. Tell us who you were actually working with, Mongrove."

Ethan scoffed at them. "Because he used mine! We worked from the same account, asshole. I tried to tell NCIS that before, but nothing could tarnish the golden boy. He was ready to sell me out! Turn me in and steal my share of the cash. He already took the job that was rightfully mine, now he fucks me over in our side business? Hell no! I knew he'd be down in Cancun and planned to lead you assholes straight to him."

The agents frowned. "And when that didn't work, you attempted to kill him in the explosion at the club."

Jett paused the video, looking back at the team. "Michael convinced the guards to let him take a meeting with Mongrove this afternoon. He slipped something in his water and then walked out the door. Fifteen minutes later, Ethan was dead." He clicked something else, and a new image of Michael flashed on the screen. There was the photo of him in uniform that they'd seen before, but as Jett clicked through the slides, there was also footage of him leaving the jail where Ethan had been held. The hair on the back of Luke's neck stood up as he took in the broad shoulders, tall stature, and bald spot at the back of the man's head.

"He was following us," Luke said, his voice steel. "He was goddamn following us."

Jett's head whipped toward him. "When?"

"A couple of weeks ago, he was at the diner when Wren and I had brunch. She said a man was watching her. Wren also mentioned that she felt uncomfortable at her studio ever since her sister's kidnapping."

"I think he was muttering something about a journalist on the surveillance footage," Jett said, suddenly looking alarmed. "Let me pull up the part of him leaving the jail."

Luke's heart stuttered, and he shoved his chair back, ignoring the loud sound it made as it fell to the floor. He shakily pulled out his phone, punching in Wren's number. It rang and rang until it went to voicemail. "Hey, call me as soon as you get this, baby. Just want to make sure everything's okay."

He tried calling her again as Sam pulled out his own phone and thumbed a text to someone, looking surprised when he got an answer. "Ava actually responded to me. She hasn't heard from Wren at all this afternoon."

Jett clicked on the video, and they could see the

back of Michael's body as he walked out, head held high. He adjusted the sound, drowning out the background noise to better hear Michael. "I'm going to make that journalist pay for messing with everything. She's mine now."

Luke's eyes locked with Jett's, who nodded at him. "Go."

"Wren," Luke growled, and then he was sprinting for the door. The fucking Marine had played them all, and his girlfriend might now be at his complete and utter mercy.

Chapter 25

Wren blinked as she woke up, feeling dizzy and disoriented. She looked around the strange bedroom, realizing she had no idea where she was. The last thing she recalled was a man forcing his way into her apartment. He'd sprayed her with something, and then everything went black. Tears smarted her eyes as she struggled to move. She was bound to the bed, her wrists tied above her head, and realized she was wearing nothing but her bra and panties. Her legs were free, but they felt heavy, the effects of whatever he'd drugged her with still coursing through her body. She started trembling, both from fear and the chill in the air, and broke out in a cold sweat. Whatever he'd given her was making her nauseous.

She whimpered as the bedroom door opened and Michael walked in, his leering gaze trailing over her body.

"I was waiting for you to wake up," he said, smiling eagerly as he stalked toward her. "I've got cameras in here watching you. Everything you do is for my eyes only. Every whimper. Every moan. You're mine now, princess."

"No," she said weakly, struggling against the restraints.

"You look good tied up," he said, licking his lips.

"No," she said again, slightly louder.

"I know you were digging into my background, naughty girl. I've got connections. You were researching me—conducting Internet searches, doing background checks. Did you think I wouldn't notice?"

"I was researching all of Ethan Mongrove's contacts. He said you were involved!" she spat out.

Michael chuckled, pulling out his cell phone. He flipped it around to show her the screen.

Ethan: *See you south of the border, Mick. I've got my plaything here. You bring the others.*

Ethan: *We'll have some fun with our new toys before we sell the goods.*

"You're Mick?" she asked in surprise, fighting harder against the restraints. "You're disgusting! How dare you kidnap those innocent girls!"

He ignored her, turning and propping his phone on the nightstand. Wren watched in horror as he aimed it directly at her. "I'm going to record this from several angles, princess. I plan to watch it again and again. Smile for the camera."

"You're sick!"

He moved away, adjusting another camera she hadn't noticed before. Michael had said he'd been watching her. Had he undressed her? She didn't think she'd been assaulted, because she wasn't sore. That brought little comfort though, because his evil intentions were clear.

"Perfect," he announced, turning back toward her.

"What are you doing?" she asked, hating the tremble in her voice.

"I'm going to take you for a ride, honey. I heard your sister was a good fuck, but I bet you've spent more time in the saddle. You can take it while I fuck you nice and hard, can't you? Then I'll let you suck me off real good."

"No," Wren whimpered, cowering away from him.

Ethan began unbuckling his belt as he moved closer.

"No!" she shouted, finding the will to kick her legs. Her movements were uncoordinated and jerky, but whatever he'd drugged her with seemed to be wearing off. Michael frowned but opened a drawer and produced a rope, wrapping it around her ankle as he tied one leg to the bed post. She shook as his gaze tracked over her again—leering. Hungry.

"You're not in control here, are you, honey?" he asked, squeezing her thigh. She kicked with her other leg, and he restrained it, so strong she knew she couldn't fight him. "I love making all the pretty girls scream. You stuck your nose where it didn't belong, took what was mine, and now we get to have a little fun. Too bad Lily's not here. Both of you at the same time would've been a fucking wet dream."

She fought against the restraints, and Michael's grip on her tightened. He reached over to the nightstand with his free hand and poured something into a glass. "Drink this like a good girl," he said, holding it to her lips.

"No," she pleaded.

He slammed the glass down, the liquid sloshing

over the sides. Rough hands squeezed her breasts as he yelled in anger, and Wren couldn't stop the tears from streaming down her cheeks. She kicked at him again, and then his large body was pinning her down. She could smell the alcohol on his breath, and as more of her senses came back online, she screamed.

Michael swore as he covered her mouth, and then suddenly, all of the lights went out.

***

Luke moved quietly toward the secluded cabin in the woods, the daylight waning. After catching a helo ride from an old military buddy of Jett's and borrowing a vehicle they left a distance away, the men were moving through the Pennsylvania forest. The last rays of the sun's light were disappearing, an ominous feeling washing over Luke. Shadows overtook the forest, and he pulled down his night vision goggles, the chill in the air creeping over his skin.

As the cabin came into view, Luke was shocked to actually see Michael's car there in plain sight. With Ethan's rental outside of Philly now compromised, Michael's cabin in the central part of the state had apparently been his second choice of location to bring victims. Was he really so arrogant he thought no one would find him? The wind shifted, the leaves rustling around Luke, but he was in the zone, focused only on the house, his gaze tracking over the property.

Several of his teammates flanked his sides as they crouched down. After Luke had torn out of the conference room, he'd rushed down to the armory to grab weapons and gear. The other guys had been hot on his heels, not letting him go alone. As they'd pulled on their Kevlar vests and comms units, West was already sending them the addresses of properties owned by Michael. The team had taken a chance heading directly to the cabin, but finally, luck was on their side. Michael's vehicle was in the driveway, and Luke's woman was being held captive inside of it.

"We've got sights on the vehicle," Sam said over the headsets. "I just confirmed the plates. That asshole is here."

"Roger that," Jett said. "Standby for another update."

A feeling of déjà vu washed over Luke as they moved closer. They'd approached a house in Mexico months ago when tracking down a missing teenager held by human traffickers. Now the woman he'd give his life for was being held by a man tied to them. Ethan and Michael had a history of trafficking girls that the military had been unaware of. They'd approached the teenagers online, set up a meeting, and taken them. It was sick and twisted, and Luke hated that they'd gotten away with it for so long. He wondered how many other victims were out there— how many others needed to be saved.

Jett's voice came over his headset. "I just spoke with one of Wren's neighbors in the city. They saw a man fitting Michael's description several hours ago. He likely went to her building and kidnapped her directly himself."

Luke clenched his jaw, speaking in a low tone. "Roger that. I don't know how the hell he got her out of that building, but I'll kill him with my bare hands if he harmed her."

Ford pointed to him, his voice filled with rage.

"We'll get your girl back."

"Damn straight," Luke said. "And then I'll rip that fucker's balls right off."

Gray's voice crackled over the headsets. "I'm on the south side of the cabin, making my approach. There are two windows but otherwise no back exits. There's no door."

"Roger. We'll have to go in through the front."

"The curtains are drawn back here," Gray said. "I can't see inside. There's a generator that's running. We could cut the power and surprise that bastard."

"Let's do it," Luke affirmed.

Nick and Ford made plans to circle the sides of the cabin, with Luke and Sam breaching the front door. They moved closer, Luke scanning the property, his finger on the trigger of his rifle. Overgrown bushes almost covered the side windows, but the front was kept clear. It was a smallish, one-story cabin. Once they entered through the front door, Michael would know they were there. They'd have mere seconds to get to Wren before he harmed her—assuming she was still alive and uninjured.

Luke choked on a breath, not wanting to even imagine the possibility of harm coming to Wren. She was so good, so innocent. He hated the thought of an evil man like Michael even breathing the same air as her, let alone touching her. Hurting her.

"I'm at the generator," Gray said in a low tone, a rustling sound coming over the headsets. "Give me a sec, and we're a go."

"Moving into position," Luke said as he and Sam jogged toward the front door.

"I'm on the eastern side," Nick said. There are no windows here, but I'll keep watch."

"I hear something," Ford said. "Western side. It might be the bedroom."

"Fuck," Luke spat out.

"Are you at the door?" Gray asked.

"Roger that," Luke said as he and Sam took their positions.

"Cutting the power in three, two, one." A woman screamed just as Gray finished his countdown, and Luke shot out the lock, he and Sam charging inside. More screams filled the otherwise quiet cabin, and Luke turned to the left, jogging down the short hallway.

"We're inside," Sam said over the headsets. "Heading to the west side. Luke's taking point."

Luke was already at the end of the hall, thankful they'd grabbed their night-vision goggles. He and his teammates could see everything in the darkened house, but Michael wouldn't be able to see anything at all. The small bathroom he'd passed had been empty, but the bedroom door was closed. Luke burst inside just as he heard glass shattering and Wren continuing to scream.

"Freeze!" Luke shouted, Sam bursting into the room behind him. "On your knees, or I'll end you right here!"

Michael was standing over Wren, a piece of broken glass in his hand. Luke briefly noticed a liquid pooling on the floor, but his heart stopped as he stared at Wren, tied to the bed. She was in her bra and panties, and Luke didn't know whether to be relieved or pissed as hell. Maybe Michel hadn't hurt her yet, but she was clearly terrified out of her mind.

The next few seconds felt like they were happening in slow motion, and as Michael lifted the shard of glass, shouting in rage, Luke aimed his rifle. He looked through the scope, centering on the asshole who'd kidnapped his woman, and then fired, the sound piercing in the small room. Michael collapsed to the ground from a single gunshot wound to the head, blood pooling on the floor. Wren continued screaming as Luke rushed over, soothing her, and Sam was already crouched beside Michael, checking for a pulse. They both knew in their gut that it was over. Luke had taken the life of the man who'd harmed so many.

"We have the package," Sam confirmed over the headsets. "Suspect is dead. House is secure. Move in."

Luke heard footsteps as his teammates came running inside, and he flipped his night vision goggles up as the power came back on. It suddenly seemed too bright, the lights showcasing the horrors of the room, but Wren crying and restrained on the bed was his only concern.

"Luke?" she whimpered, tears streaming down her face as she looked up at him.

His gloved hand brushed some of her hair back, and his lips touched her forehead. Her skin felt cold and clammy, but her floral scent teasing his nostrils reminded him that she was the sweetest damn thing he'd ever known. Luke wanted to kill the bastard who'd hurt her all over again, punishing him for threatening and terrifying his girl.

"You're safe now. Let me get you out of these." Luke was already pulling out a knife, cutting her free from the restraints. Wren was shaking, and he wrapped her in the sheet, pulling her tight against his body. He heard his teammates moving around the room, dragging Michael's body out and taking note of the cameras. His arms tightened around Wren as she buried her face in his chest. She was everything to him, and he'd nearly lost her.

"Is he dead?" she asked, choking on her tears.

"It's over, baby. I got you. I got you," he soothed, holding her so tightly, he didn't think he'd ever be able to let go.

Epilogue

One Month Later

Wren crossed her small studio, setting the pile of books into the large moving box. Luke came out from behind the closet doors, looking boyishly charming in the baseball cap he'd pulled on with his tee shirt and jeans. His muscles bulged from the heavy load he was carrying, and she smiled, wondering how the hell she'd gotten so lucky.

"How many clothes do you have, woman?" Luke joked, winking as he set the box he'd been carrying down on the floor. "Your closet is still crammed full of stuff."

"Not nearly enough," she said. "Do you have any idea how amazing the shopping is in the city?"

He burst into laughter, scrubbing a hand over his jaw. "Nope. Can't say I do."

A truck honked on the city streets below, and her gaze tracked to the open window. "I hope that's not Ford," she said with a frown.

"Nah, he's not here with the truck yet. Sam went downstairs to keep the loading area clear for us. He'll text me when the truck's here. I've got a dolly set aside for the guys and me to haul down your furniture. In a couple of hours, this place will be empty."

"I can't believe we're really doing this," she said excitedly, stretching up on her toes to kiss him. Luke's arms immediately wrapped around her, and he held her close as his lips moved over hers.

"Ew, get a room," Ava teased as she walked inside Wren's studio.

Luke waggled his eyebrows as he released Wren. "Duh. We are. Your best friend finally came to her senses and agreed to move in with me."

"Finally?" Ava asked with laugh. "You two have been dating like two seconds. I'd say that's fast." She took a sip of water, the amusement still clear on her face.

Wren shook her head. "Two months. Apparently, that was slow as far as this group is concerned."

Ava made a face, looking over at her. "It was fast, sister. I'm going to miss you so much! Who am I supposed to hang out with in the city now?"

"Girl, you travel all the time!" Wren said, giving her bestie a quick hug. "We barely see each other now because you're so busy jetting all over the world."

"Yeah, yeah. All right. I'll come visit you upstate I guess when I'm here in town. Now, put me to work so you can move in with your man today."

"Um…." Wren worried her lip, looking around with a frown. "Kitchen? I've barely made a dent in there."

"It's all under control," Ava assured her, grabbing

an empty box and crossing the small studio to the kitchen area.

Wren walked back to the packed closet beside her bed, pulling more garments out and tossing them into a box. Luke was opening one of her dresser drawers and chuckled. "Jackpot," he murmured, and she flushed as he pulled out a lacy negligee. "You know what this reminds me of," he said huskily.

Her heart raced as he held the red lace in his big hand, heat washing over her face. Wren had worn that last weekend when Luke had gotten back from an op. He'd bent her over the bed, pushing the lace aside, and eaten her out from behind. When she'd been fisting the sheets and crying out his name, her pussy spasming, he'd moved away and then slid inside her, filling her to the brink with his thick cock as he'd claimed her. Luke had made her come once more before finally exploding himself. He held himself behind her afterwards, peppering her with kisses as he murmured sweet words.

"I might have an idea," she said, watching as his lips quirked.

He moved closer and ducked for a brief kiss. "Best welcome home ever," he joked. He trailed his fingers over her cheek. "I still love how you blush for me."

"Yeah. I think I've noticed that."

His lips quirked, but it was the affection in his eyes that made her heart flutter. "I'm happy as hell that you're moving in with me. I thought I lost you a month ago," he said, his deep voice filling the empty spaces inside of her, warming her until she thought she might burst. "I can't imagine my life without you in it."

"Luke," she whispered.

"I still have nightmares about when you were kidnapped but thank God every day that you're mine. I love you," he said huskily, and then he was kissing her again, stealing her breath.

"I love you, too," she said as he finally pulled away, their eyes locking. It felt like she and Luke were the only two people in the world. He'd faced down monsters to save both her and her sister, and she couldn't imagine not having this incredible man in her life.

"Knock, knock," a deep voice said, and then Sam was striding inside, his large frame looking huge in her small space. He glanced over, stilling as he realized Ava was in Wren's kitchen. "Ava," he said with a nod.

She'd frozen in place, her face paling, then blew out an exasperated breath.

"So we're still not talking, I see," he quipped.

"How about you both call a truce for today," Wren said as she walked over. "Let's get everything packed up and out of here."

"Ford's on his way," Sam said. "He just texted his ETA is five minutes out. I came up to grab some water." He moved to the kitchen, Ava stiffening as Sam took a water bottle from the fridge, his large body beside hers. Wren's eyes shifted between the two of them, and then Ava relaxed and walked toward her.

"Oh, you know how we were talking about traveling? I forgot to tell you my news. I'm going to Cairo!" Ava excitedly announced. "I've been commissioned to do some sculptures and will be living there for the summer."

"Really? That's amazing!" Wren said, giving her

best friend a hug. "When did you find out?"

"I just finalized it yesterday. You've been busy with plans for your move, so I hadn't gotten a chance to mention it yet."

"Cairo?" Sam asked, whipping his head around. The cap from the water bottle fell to the floor, and Wren noticed he was gripping the plastic bottle more tightly than necessary. Concern etched across his face.

"Oh, you heard that? I thought you only responded when we were in bed together."

"Ava," he ground out.

"You should come visit!" Ava continued, ignoring Sam. "Write a story about Egypt or something. Think about how much fun we'd have."

"Well, maybe," Wren said, biting her lip. "I'll have to see."

"Think about it," Ava insisted. "I'll be there several months. You can come for a week or two. We can explore together and take a tour. It'll be fantastic. I'll get to show you the pieces I'm working on, too."

Sam was still frowning as his phone buzzed, and he glanced back up at the two of them. "Who commissioned you to do this artwork?" he asked.

"Oh, some businessman. I have all the info in an email. I signed the contract agreeing to the work and just need to get my plane tickets. He'll reimburse me for the cost."

"And you didn't research the guy?" Sam asked in disbelief.

"It'll be fine," she insisted. "Don't rain on my parade, buddy. You worry about your own life, and I'll worry about mine. You certainly had no interest in it until we oh-so-unfortunately ran into each other again."

"Ford's here," Luke interrupted, glancing down at his phone. "Why don't Sam and I start moving the furniture with him while you ladies finish packing?"

"Sounds good!" Wren said, flashing a curious look at Sam. He still looked irritated for some reason, but Ava had already headed back to the kitchen and was stacking plates.

Luke pressed a kiss on Wren's temple, smiling. "Let's get this show on the road then. I've got big plans for our first night living together."

"Oh yeah?" she asked.

"Absolutely," he said with a grin, and heat filled her cheeks. He brushed a piece of her hair back, looking into her eyes as Sam and Ava started bickering about packing up the kitchen.

"I love you, Wren Martin," Luke said huskily. "Who would've thought I'd meet a journalist in Mexico and move her into my place because I can't stand the idea of being apart a single night?"

"Not me," she promptly said. "I didn't even like you at first."

He burst out laughing, ducking down for a sweet kiss. "Thank God you changed your mind. I can't imagine my life without you in it."

"Me either, baby," she whispered, and he pulled her close, kissing her deeply amidst the stacks of boxes, their life together just beginning.

About the Author

USA Today Bestselling Author Makenna Jameison writes sizzling romantic suspense, including the addictive Alpha SEALs series.

Makenna loves the beach, strong coffee, red wine, and traveling. She lives in Washington DC with her husband and two daughters.

Visit www.makennajameison.com to discover your next great read.

Manufactured by Amazon.ca
Acheson, AB

16885227R00141